The War on Wildlife

by Steven W. Krull

Copyright 2026 Steven W. Krull
All Rights Reserved

No part of this book may be reproduced or stored in a retrieval system, or transmitted in any form or by any means, electronic, mechanical, photocopying, recording, or otherwise without express written permission of the publisher.

ISBN: 979-8-9860766-6-9

Cover design by Steven W. Krull
Printed in the United States of America

Table of Contents

Preface

The *War On Wildlife* is the third in a trilogy of historical fiction romantic adventure novels, as experienced by an interesting and eclectic set of characters who's lives weave a tale of education, adventure, courage, and of course love and loss, as they dedicate their lives to preserving America's iconic wildlife against all odds.

This book and it's prequels, *Spirit of the Wolf* and *Thundering Hooves* will both entertain and inspire readers as they learn the true history of wildlife conservation in America, from the introduction of wolves in Yellowstone, to the rescue of the Sand Wash Basin wild mustang herd in western Colorado, and finally the real life saga of tragedy and triumph as Colorado attempts to establish a wolf population a century after their extinction in the 20th century.

Prologue

The War on Wildlife begins in tumultuous times. Colorado voters passed ballot measure 114 in the 2020 elections, mandating Colorado Parks and Wildlife to introduce wolves to the mountain ecosystem in the state's remote wilderness. On the flip side, the new Democrat presidential administration decided to double down on the treachery of the previous administration by defending the removal of wolves from the Endangered Species List, and returning wolf management to the discretion of the states. The immediate result of that decision was an unprecedented slaughter of wolves nationwide that ultimately deprived Yellowstone National Park of a third of it's beloved wolf population.

As this story begins, America was starting to find it's way back from the pandemic and people were finally going back to work. Many faced returning to jobs that no longer existed, and some discovered that times had changed and others had taken their place in the work force.

Eventually protection for wolves was restored in 2022 by a federal judge, but the gray wolves of the Rocky Mountain West were exempted from the ruling. Old hatred of the predator boiled over, and the western states of Wyoming, Montana, and Idaho resumed the systematic slaughter that brought the animals to near extinction in the early 1900's. The Bureau of Land Management learned little from the outcry of Colorado voters and the governor over the destruction of the Sand Wash mustang herd, and continued it's abhorrent practice of helicopter roundups throughout the west, including several ranges in Colorado.

It is in this setting that the third in the trilogy, *The War on Wildlife* begins. The main characters, Caleb, Angie and Michelle are struggling to make new lives following the massive mustang roundup that ended the previous story in this wildlife series.

The previous book, *Thundering Hooves* ended with the trio camped out in western Colorado at the end of a major roundup. Angie and Michelle had drifted off to sleep, mesmerized by the flickering flames of the campfire while Caleb remained awake, reflecting on the day's action as the glowing embers grew cold along with the final vestiges of summer.

Introduction

In every war there are warriors, heroes, exciting stories, and of course victims. Through my first two books in a series of historical fiction novels, Caleb, Lacey, Angie and Michelle have steadfastly done their best to protect and preserve some of America's most iconic wild creatures. In doing so, they have experienced countless adventures, romance, love, danger, and inevitable heartbreak and loss.

The series begins with the book *Spirit of the Wolf*, when Caleb enrolls in the photography curriculum at a college in the Bay Area of California. It is there that he meets the love of his life and begins a career in fashion photography, as his love Lacey launches a successful career as a fashion model. Find out if their romance can survive as Lacey hits the big time, and Caleb hears the call of the wild and the mournful howl of the wolf in faraway Yellowstone National Park.

Angie is a bartender at a popular microbrew in Bozeman, Montana. She doesn't realize it yet, but her life will soon take a dramatic turn when the adventurous Caleb rolls into town hoping to learn more about a famous female gray wolf that has captured the hearts of many with her courageous leadership of the Lamar Pack in Yellowstone National Park.

At the famous Roosevelt entrance to Yellowstone National Park in Gardiner, Montana, Michelle is still in high school, working hard at a local coffee shop to save money for college. She is inspired by the dashing Caleb, as he often stops in for coffee on his way to exciting adventures with the wolf packs in the park. She too is unaware of the important part she will play in the exciting and often dangerous war being waged by ranchers and hunters against the beloved wolf packs in the park and surrounding wilderness of Montana, Wyoming and Idaho.

In *Thundering Hooves*, the second in the wildlife series, the intrepid group learns of a terrifying plot by ranchers and sheep herders to rid the land of a magnificent herd of wild horses and it's patriarch, a stallion revered and followed by horse lovers all over the world. After launching a successful wildlife protection movement in Montana, will the tireless trio be able to save the iconic herd of mustangs from the infamous slaughter houses of Mexico? Through more exciting tales of romance, adventure and danger, learn the real life story of the Sand Wash Basin mustang herd as the entire state of Colorado comes together to stop a national outrage.

The wildlife advocacy group's tireless work has helped to save countless animals and thousands of acres of important wilderness, but the war continues unabated as Colorado voters approve the reintroduction of wolves into the Rocky Mountains of western Colorado. Ranchers and hunting outfitters rage against the new arrivals to the state, and without intervention they will surely destroy the new wolf packs before they ever get a chance to thrive.

Follow our main characters as they navigate life's challenges while undertaking a dangerous battle against greedy special interests who continue their constant efforts to kill anything or anyone that gets in the way of profit and unbridled lust for blood and death. *The War on Wildlife* is ongoing in real life, as the new Republican administration climbs into bed with western politicians who are determined to resume the wanton killing of the 19th and 20th centuries that threatened to slaughter wild wolves of the west to extinction.

My new book, *The War on Wildlife* will bring to light the nefarious backroom deals that threaten to destroy our beloved parks and national forest land at the behest of a small minority of the American population that is unable to leave the 19th century behind, and accept a new way of life where Americans from all walks of life are able to enjoy the magnificent landscape and diverse wildlife of the Rocky Mountain West.

The Intrepid Trio

Angie was awakened early on a beautiful sunny Colorado autumn morning by the gurgling of the coffee pot in the kitchen. She had set her alarm for 6:30 in the morning., leaving plenty of time to put on her makeup for a meeting at the real estate office. However, Caleb was perpetually the early riser and had already turned it on. Some new home sales listings in Douglas County had recently become available, and she hoped to land one of the assignments. It would be a busy day, as she also had a go-see scheduled in the afternoon for her modeling agency.

Caleb as always was already sitting at the kitchen table, sipping a cup of the aromatic brew as his tall slender blonde bride strode into the room. "Morning Ang, how are you this morning?"

"I'll be better once I get a cup of this coffee down!"

"I know how you feel."

Angie asked, "What do you have going today?"

"I'm on a roll with my book. I think a few more days and I should have *Thundering Hooves* ready to publish. What are you doing up so early?"

"Oh, I have a couple of meetings today, one at the real estate office and a go-see for the modeling agency."

"I'm sure you'll knock them dead."

"I don't know, everything has changed since the pandemic."

"Don't worry about it, just go in and be yourself. You'll do just fine, just like always."

"I don't know, we'll see."

Angie poured herself a cup of java and sat down as morning sunshine streamed through the kitchen window. Caleb asked, "Are you going to be around awhile before you have to go?"

"No, I'm just going to drink this and get dressed for the meeting."

"Okay, I think I'll go for a little run in the canyon to clear my head before I try to start writing."

Angie replied, "That sounds like fun. I'll see you later then."

As Angie sipped her coffee, a slightly disheveled Michelle walked into the room.

Angie laughed and asked, "Late night?"

"Yeah, me and some of the parks people were having drinks and got to talking about the wolf release. I might have had a couple extra drinks," she said as she fluffed her long blonde hair.

"How is the wolf release coming along anyway?"

"Really well I think! Parks has sourced a pack of wolves from Oregon and we hope to release them up near the Sand Wash sometime in the winter."

"Are you going to be there when they let them go?"

"Well, that's what we were talking about. Everyone wants to be on the release team."

"But you are going to apply right?"

"Do you think I should? There are a lot more senior officers than me who want to be on it."

"True, but how many of them were a federal park ranger in Yellowstone? You have actual experience with wild wolves."

"That's a good point I guess. I suppose I might as well go ahead and throw my hat in the ring!"

"Awesome! Caleb will be so excited if you actually made the

release team."

Michelle chuckled and replied, "I know, he'll never stop tormenting me for the location if I get in."

"I'll set him straight if he gets to be a pain," Angie said with a smile.

Michelle laughed and said, "You might be the only one on the planet who can reign him in!"

Michelle smiled wryly and said, "We go way back. If you think he's out of control now, you should have known him when he first got to Bozeman!"

"Oh I remember, he got into a fight with some wolf hunters at the coffee shop in Gardiner one time."

Angie chuckled and answered, "I remember that. What are you doing today?"

"It's one of my days to man the north gate into the canyon. So it's going to be boring day, but I'm looking forward to just staring at the scenery and drinking coffee."

"Do they have a coffee pot in the hut?"

"No, I'll have to take some in my insulated mug."

Caleb finally joined the conversation and said, "Maybe I'll stop in at the hut and chat for a while. I'm going out to run the trails pretty soon."

"That would be great Caleb, I'll be just sitting there by myself. Nobody hardly ever shows up on a Monday."

Angie gulped down the last of her coffee and grabbed her purse. As she went out the door she said, "Well you two have fun in the canyon. I'm off to my meetings."

Michelle yelled through the closing door, "Good luck today!"

Caleb and Michelle looked out the window and heard a faint reply, "Thanks!"

Michelle asked Caleb, "Are you done in the bathroom. I'm going to take a shower."

"I'm done, all I have to do is lace up and head out the back door. Lock up when you leave, okay?"

"Sure," Michelle replied.

Caleb slipped through the sliding glass door onto the back deck and walked onto the barren rocks of the rocky plateau on the east side of Castlewood Canyon State Park. He pondered his book manuscript as he began jogging slowly toward the trail down into the canyon at the north end of the park. He knew Michelle wouldn't be there yet, but he would catch her on his second lap around the figure eight trail system.

Michelle decided on a soak instead of a shower, and maneuvered her diminutive frame into the tub and slid down into the hot water. As the warm water soothed her lean muscles, her thoughts turned to her mother in Montana, whom she had left behind many months before. She had always believed she would never leave Gardiner, but her friendship with Caleb had paved the way for an escape. Caleb too, would still be in Montana were it not for Angie taking her shot at a real estate career in Denver. She thought to herself how amazing it was how all this had come together, and how she was now living with close friends she thought she'd never see again.

Angie made the turn onto highway 83 towards her real estate office in Parker, her eyes glued to the road. It had been awhile since she had earned a good commission, and she was worried that today the losing streak would continue. Regardless, she would go through the motions and do her best to convince management that she was the best candidate to sell one of the new listings. The parking lot was almost full by the time Angie arrived at town square in Parker, but she was able to find a spot in the shopping center across the street. She knew she wouldn't be in town long enough for her car to attract attention, and it was just a short walk across the street to the real estate office.

Jennifer greeted her as she walked through the door, "Good Morning Angie, how are you today?"

"I'm well, how about yourself?"

Laughing, Jennifer answered, "Oh you know, living the dream!"

"Isn't that the truth. Are the others already in the conference room?"

"Not everyone is here yet, but there's coffee and donuts."

"Oh boy, sounds like bad news," responded Angie.

Angie noticed a number of new faces as she entered the room. However, she was tired and not in a mood to meet new people, and especially not up to making new friends. She poured herself a cup of coffee and snagged a donut before finding a seat near the front of the big conference table. She felt a twinge of resentment as the new people laughed and joked with each other.

Brenda the office manager eventually strode through the door and took her place at the head of the table. Angie watched carefully for any sign that might indicate the tone of the gathering.

Speaking sternly, Brenda finally said, "Let's take our seats everyone."

The laughing quieted to quiet muttering as the sound of chairs being dragged into place filled the room. Soon everyone's attention was focused on the the boss lady.

"Okay, the good news is that we have some new listings to assign. The bad news is there aren't enough contracts for everyone. However, business is picking up after the pandemic and I'm sure that soon there will be plenty of work for all of you."

Brenda picked up a stack of papers and handed them to a new agent sitting next to her.

“I have here a sheet with the new properties associated with a sales agent. Please take one and pass them around the room.”

Angie took one of the papers from the top of the stack and passed them to the person next to her. She searched for her name, and was stunned to see that junior agents were assigned to listings she was better qualified to sell.

“Any questions?” asked Brenda.

Angie responded, “I see that a couple of these are right in my neighborhood. I know these people personally and I don't understand why I wasn't given first choice on these. And why are junior agents getting listings ahead of some of us who have been here for years?”

“As you all know, the newly elected Dolittle administration has made it clear that diversity and equity are a high priority, as defined in his new DE& I executive order. I'm sorry if you feel it isn't fair to some of you, but we feel some fresh faces are needed in our firm to show a spirit of cooperation.”

Angie asked, “So what are the quota numbers that we are required to adhere to?”

“There is no set quota, and we are just taking one step at a time to see how we can adapt to the new reality.”

Angie bitterly responded, “So you don't really have to do this, you just want to.”

“After the last four years of threats to our democracy, we just feel that change is welcome.”

Robert, another long time employee chimed in, “Aren't you worried that your best agents are going to go out on their own and compete with you?”

“We've considered that, and feel that the risk to our firm is low.”

The room then descended into chaos and Angie rose stiffly to her feet and walked out without speaking to anyone. Her mind was spinning as she wondered how she might go into business on her own. She thought to herself, "*I wonder how much advertising would cost to compete with them? What about insurance, and how will I be able to travel around showing homes without a salary to cover the cost of transportation?*"

She took her bag into the restroom to shed her drab business attire for a sexier outfit befitting a model at a go-see. The sun was shining brightly, and by this time she could feel the heat emanating from the black asphalt. She was careful not to work up a sweat on her way to the car, and turned the air conditioning on full blast for the long drive downtown.

Back in Franktown, Michelle examined her minimal makeup and hair in the mirror as she put on her park officer's uniform. "*Good enough for the guard shack,*" she thought to herself. She put some snacks and drinks in her backpack and checked to see that the stove and coffee pot were turned off. Caleb was already gone, so she locked the sliding doors and departed through the big double doors in front.

Soon she was parked at the front entrance to the state park, and took her place in the office chair provided for the rangers. There were no visitors there to get day passes yet, so she took a deep breath and looked over the beautiful scenery of this hidden gem of a park that few were aware of. She pulled a novel out of her pack to help pass the time between visitors.

Her eyes grew heavy after a couple hours of boredom and just as she was about to fall asleep, a state car pulled up. "*I wonder what they want?*" she asked herself.

She quickly recognized her friend Heather, who had a big smile on her face as she approached. Michelle greeted her with a smile, saying, "Hey Heather, what brings you down to my neck of the woods this fine morning?"

"I just came down to congratulate you."

"Oh, what did I do?"

"Well as it turns out, I put you in for the wolf release team and you are officially approved! You were a shoe in with your Yellowstone experience. Nobody even questioned it, they just nodded when your name came up."

"Awesome, I'm so excited! When is it going to be? We don't even have any wolves yet do we?"

"Not yet, but we are close to an agreement with Oregon for a few specimens. We are hoping to have them ready to release sometime early in the winter. Perhaps before the holidays."

"Oh, I can't wait to tell Caleb. He's been talking about this ever since he heard about the ballot measure."

"Well okay, you can tell him but make sure he understands nothing has been finalized yet. And tell him not to write about it yet."

"I'll let him know to keep it to himself until there's public confirmation."

Heather reached out to give Michelle a hug and congratulated her again, "Well, I need to get going, but I wanted to be the first to let you know about the wolf release."

"Thank you so much, I am so excited! Okay, you have a great day Heather!"

"I will."

Moonlight Dance

Deep in the Oregon rain forest a thousand miles away, an ancient dance was playing out in the moonlight. Ember, a two year old gray wolf was becoming restless as all female wolves do as they approach adulthood. Until recently she had been content with her place in the Aspen Butte Pack, happily going out on hunts by day, and playing and napping with her siblings after feeding time in the evening. Now though, she was feeling urges she didn't yet understand. There was a yearning for something new, an urge that her siblings could no longer satiate. She found herself going off by herself during the day, returning only to sleep within the safety of her pack at night.

One bright morning she was awakened by a lonesome howl in the distance, a sound she would have normally considered a threat to her family. But on this morning she felt strangely drawn to investigate, and once again headed out on her own. Her siblings looked on with great curiosity as she trotted into the dense forest alone. After a few minutes she stopped and returned the strange howl with a call of her own. She continued in the direction of the peculiar communication, and soon heard another bark as the other wolf beckoned her to approach. Soon Ember saw the big male trot into a clearing, and she watched intently as he stopped and stared back at her. Shadow was about the same age as Ember, and was also in the process of dispersing from his natal pack.

Ember was instantly attracted to her powerful suitor, and struck a submissive pose indicating that she welcomed his presence, and would not attack. He tentatively moved in closer as she lay down to await his arrival. With tails wagging, the two wolves greeted each other, first with sniffing and then with more intimate face licking. Soon the new couple was frolicking in the grass and a bond had been formed for life. Shadow and Ember would eventually mate and form the nucleus of a new pack.

Ember gestured for Shadow to follow her as she headed back toward her natal pack. He had no intention of letting his new prize get away, and followed without question. Soon Ember came into the view of her old pack and let out a bark to attract their attention. Normally a pack will not allow a strange wolf to enter their territory, however they seemed to understand what was transpiring. Shadow didn't attempt to approach the Aspen Butte pack members and they didn't threaten him. When Ember turned to depart, her family understood that her time had come to break the bond, and she was now in the care of her new mate.

The Aspen Butte Pack howled their goodbyes as Shadow and Ember disappeared into the dense pine forest, joyfully running side by side. The new pair instinctively knew that they needed to put some distance between themselves and Ember's family. They needed their privacy and they needed fresh hunting territory, away from competition with her siblings. Thus is the circle of life for gray wolves in the wilderness of the Great Northwest.

Wolves were the furthest thing from Angie's mind as she drove north on I25 toward the Merchandise Center, where she would meet her agency at the location of an upcoming fashion show and merchandise sale. She continued to fume over her treatment at the real estate meeting, as she negotiated heavy downtown Denver traffic. She thought to herself, "*At least I still have my modeling to fall back on. I don't need those jerks, and I don't even like selling houses.*"

The traffic and tall buildings of downtown Denver were soon in Angie's rear view mirror, and she was rapidly approaching her exit from I25 onto 58th Avenue. She quickly found a parking place and went in to meet the fashion show organizers. As she approached, she recognized a couple of the models from her agency that she had worked with before. Amanda the booking agent was already there, talking to an important looking middle aged man in a suit and tie. Angie surmised he must be the fashion show coordinator.

She strode up to the gathering and greeted Amanda who then introduced her to Tristan, the man in the suit.

"Tristan, this is Angie, Angie Tristan. Angie is one of our top runway models that we will be presenting for your approval today."

He responded with a smile, "Hi Angie, it's nice to meet you!"

"Likewise!" she responded enthusiastically.

He added, "It looks like we have quite a few models here already, so I think we'll get started. Angie, why don't you go ahead and jump in behind the group that has already gathered back by the curtain."

"Sure!"

Angie took her place with the others, and Tristan motioned for the first model to enter the catwalk. Angie looked around at the growing group of models while thinking to herself, "*How did these girls even get accepted by the agency? They look more like the hired help than models. Since when did we start including such sloppy looking applicants*?" She watched as the first one practically ran down the catwalk. It was obvious that she had no training, and didn't walk like a professional model at all. The catwalk shook and her footsteps echoed throughout the big room.

Angie's friend Jessica was next, gracefully making her down the catwalk where she made a perfect turn at the end, and returned equally as gracefully. Jessica had joined the agency about the same time as Angie, and was tall and slender with beautiful flowing brunette colored hair with streaks of golden blonde. One by one each model took a turn and soon

Angie's opportunity drew near..

Finally, the model right before her clumsily walked down the runway and Angie wondered, "*How is that look supposed to sell these clothes?*"

Angie was prepared when her turn came, and entered the runway just as the previous model finished her walk. She had been practicing the catwalk since she was a young girl, when she and her sister would put on imaginary shows at their home in Gardiner, Montana. She gracefully swayed down the shining floor, beautiful smile radiating brightly with her long hair blowing lightly in the breeze produced by the fan. She paused at the end to perform a stunning final pose before whirling around and confidently striding back to the curtain.

"*I nailed that!*" she thought to herself.

Tristan took the microphone and said, "Thank you to all of you ladies. Give Amanda and I a few minutes to talk it over, and we'll give you an answer in a few minutes. We will be selecting eight of you for the show, while the rest will be kept on file for future engagements."

Angie and Jessica sat down together in the audience chairs to await the results. Jessica commented, "Can you believe some of these models? I don't know when they took on this new bunch, but they sure didn't have to go through the same acceptance process that we endured."

"No, I don't know what is going on. Standards must have been relaxed for the new equity push, but I don't see how it sells high fashion clothing."

Jessica asked, "So what do you think of this Tristan guy? I've never seen him before."

"I don't know, he seems just like all the other's that we have worked with. He seems nice enough."

Angie exclaimed, "Oh, here they come. Good, I want to get this over with. I have other things I need to do today!"

Tristan took the microphone again and began to speak, "Okay, these are the eight models we would like to represent us in the show."

He read a list of eight names, none of which included Angie or Jessica. The two shocked women sat motionless in their chairs, stunned at the finality of the announcement.

Eventually Angie regained her composure and said, "Can you believe this?"

"No, I can't," replied Jessica.

"Let's go talk to Amanda," said Angie.

"Okay yeah, let's find out what is going on."

Angie and Jessica approached a sheepish looking Amanda, and didn't even need to ask a question before she started explaining, "I don't know what to say girls. I'm as surprised as you are."

Jessica responded, "But you must know something. You had to accept these models into our agency."

"Well, all I know is that times have changed with the election of the new administration, fashion is taking on a more inclusive look. I strongly recommended you two to Tristan, but he was mumbling something about tall skinny girls being some kind of trigger. He's afraid of backlash if his show isn't diverse enough."

Angie responded, "Well damn, doesn't that beat all. So is this the way it's going to be from now on?"

Amanda answered, "I don't know, I'm not very good at predicting the future."

Jessica answered, "Well you were good enough at telling the future to know to hire these sloppy looking models."

Amanda shrugged her shoulders and said, "I don't know, we'll have to just see how it plays out."

Angie and Jessica turned and walked toward the exit.

Angie asked Jessica, "Do you want to get a drink somewhere?"

"Yeah, where do you want to go?"

"How about that little place with the aquariums on Arapaho Road, what's the name of it? That cool little sports bar. I think it's JR's or something like that. East Arapahoe is on your way home right?"

"Sure I know that place, it sounds great. Do you want to just meet there?"

"Yeah, whoever gets there first can go in and get a table. I love just watching those fish swim around. It seems relaxing to me."

"Okay, I'll see you there."

Angie followed Jessica out of the parking lot, but lost her on 58th

Avenue prior to turning onto the freeway. "*No worries she thought to herself, we'll meet up at the bar.*"

It seemed dark in the bar when Angie walked in. She squinted her eyes and looked around the room for her friend, finally spotting her near the back of the big dining room. She stepped down through the center area and up the steps onto to the raised dining area in the back.

"I figured you'd want a glass of wine so I went ahead and ordered for us."

"That's awesome, thank you Jessica!"

"I also have some nachos on the way to help with our mood."

"Nachos sound great! Man, could you believe those new girls?"

"I know, they were stomping down the catwalk I thought it was going to collapse."

"I know right?"

Jessica laughed so hard she got tears in her eyes.

Angie was having a good laugh as well and added, "Oh my God, my sides hurt!"

A few minutes later after the two women had gained their composure Angie commented, "I think this is just what we needed, a good laugh. What are we going to do about these changes?"

Jessica replied, "Can you imagine what they would have said if we showed up looking like that when we first applied?"

"I can't imagine, and all that time and work in the gym, all the dieting and starving, and for what?"

"I don't know anymore. Surely this trend can't last, can it?"

Angie replied, "I can't imagine everyone is buying into this new idea of inclusiveness for anyone who thinks they should get to do anything, qualified or not. Although I just had the same experience this morning at the real estate agency. They say they need new faces, a new look."

"Yeah, a hideous look."

"After this morning's meeting I was thinking of going out on my own in real estate, but I don't really want to sell houses. And I especially don't want the hassle of running my own real estate agency. I just don't need that kind of stress."

Jessica replied, "Maybe we could go out on our own as models."

"I guess we could try our hand at Instapix. Caleb is a photographer and I suppose he could get me started."

"You are lucky, you have a photographer. I don't know who I could get to shoot my pictures."

"Caleb would probably be happy to shoot for both of us. He's always trying to get me to pose for his stock photo library."

"Really, you don't think he would mind?"

"No really, when I'm too busy to pose he just goes out on his own and shoots anything else he can find. He does a lot of sports, wildlife and landscape photography just to have something to upload to his agency. I don't think he really cares much about what he's shooting on any particular day."

"Well that sounds great then, we should do it!"

Angie reached out to shake Jessica's hand and said, "Yeah, let's give it a try! We don't need those bitches down at the agency. I'll talk to Caleb tomorrow."

Jessica added, "We've been carrying that place for too long. Maybe they will go out of business."

"I hope so."

The two women sat and talked and sipped wine for a couple hours while they talked over their new idea. Soon they had worked out a general business plan that would be the basis for their new venture.

Eventually the new business partners grew weary and Angie said, "I'd better get home. Caleb is probably starting to wonder where I am. In fact I guess I should send him a text."

"Yeah, me too. Call me tomorrow, and maybe we can come up with a name for our new business."

"I know Caleb managed to get a trademark for his ex girlfriend Lacey for her outdoor fashion company. Maybe he can design and register one for us too."

"That would be awesome! Okay, I'll talk to you tomorrow."

“Watch out for the cops!” laughed Angie.

“Oh I will. I'm going to stick to the back roads just in case.”

“Good idea.”

They each climbed into their cars and parted ways for the night, their minds racing at the idea of starting their own fashion company.

Caleb the Anchor

Fresh brewed coffee awaited Caleb as he walked into a cold room just as the first rays of sunshine streamed through the kitchen window. Michelle was the next to awaken, excited to tell Caleb the good news of her appointment to the wolf release team.

Caleb greeted Michelle with a cheery, “Good morning sunshine!”

“Oh My God Caleb, you are not going to believe this!”

“What?”

“Heather stopped by yesterday with some great news!”

“What news?” laughed Caleb. “Spit it out woman!”

Michelle laughed too, “Heather stopped by while I was at the booth yesterday to let me know that I've been selected for the wolf release team!”

“That's amazing Michelle! When is it going to be, and where?”

“Whoa, hold your horses big boy! She told me that nothing is in stone yet, but they might have a source for wolves, and that the release might be before the end of the year. But she also told me to tell you specifically not to write about it yet.”

Laughing, Caleb replied “Don't worry, I'll keep your secret!”

“I'm sure you will be one of the first to know, when the information becomes available.”

"Do you think there's any chance I might get to be there to film the release?"

"I don't know, but I'll put in a good word for you every time I get a chance!"

"Thanks Michelle, I appreciate that."

Michelle poured most of the remaining coffee in the pot into her insulated cup and said, "I've got to get to work, I hope it's okay if I take all the coffee!"

"Don't worry about it, I'm sure I can grind some more. Have a great day at work!"

"I'll try!"

Just as Michelle closed the door, a slightly hung over Angie walked into the kitchen and asked if there was any coffee left.

Caleb replied, "Michelle just took most of it, but there's probably a half a cup left. I can have a new pot brewing by the time you finish that."

"Okay, thanks Caleb."

"How did all your meetings go yesterday?"

"Not too well I'm afraid. Seems the pandemic and the new administration have managed to change everything."

"What do you mean, everything?"

“I mean everything. Suddenly tall blondes seem to be enemy number one. First the real estate agency tells me I'm no longer the face they want representing the agency. They even gave my local listings here in Douglas County to new people. Then I heard pretty much the same story at the modeling go-see up in Denver. Jessica and I were both rejected. Apparently we have become some kind of trigger for people who don't take care of themselves.”

“What are you going to do?”

“Well, Jessie and I went out for a few drinks and talked it over. We are going to start our own fashion company, starting with becoming influencers on Instapix. We were wondering if you would mind taking us out on a few photo shoots to help us get started?”

“Sure, no problem, Jessica too?”

“She was hoping you wouldn't mind.”

“No problem, do you think she would mind signing a model release so I can use the pictures for my business too?”

“I'm sure she wouldn't mind.”

“I've been wanting to get back out the the Sand Wash before winter. What do you think about doing a western style photoshoot with the horses like we did last year?”

“That would be fun, I would like that!”

“Maybe we could stay in Steamboat on the way back and do a more high fashion shoot there.”

“That's a great idea Caleb, I'll see if Jessica wants to come.”

“Do you really think she would want to go camping? She seems a bit girly to me.”

Angie burst out laughing, “You just know her when she's modeling, she's a lot tougher than you might think.”

Caleb chuckled and replied, “I didn't mean anything. She will be a great partner for you in your new endeavor. Are you just going to model, or are you going into designing as well?”

“We haven't gotten that far yet, we just got the idea yesterday. That reminds me of something we talked about. I remember you said you got Lacey a trademark. Do you think you could design one for us as well?”

“Sure, I don't think that would be a problem. It takes forever to get one though, but the good news is you can use the mark while it is pending. So whatever we can come up with, you can put a TM by it to indicate you are pending registration.”

“Cool, I'll let Jessie know and see if she wants to go to the Sand Wash. What are you going to do today?”

“I'm getting close to publishing *Thundering Hooves,* so I guess I'll start my final review and tidy up the introduction and epilogue.”

“Good, I can't wait to see it! I'm supposed to meet Jessie for lunch so we can make plans. By the way, how did Lacey get her clothing line started?”

“I don't exactly know. Of course she had her fashion degree from school in California, so I imagine that gave her a head start. But I know she had to make a lot of phone calls to find suppliers for all the materials, and in some cases she just bought finished product from companies and put her logo on them."

"Sounds like a lot of work!"

"It was, but you and Jessie have a great sense of fashion, and your modeling experience will be invaluable in marketing new products."

Angie excitedly replied, "Oh, this is gong to be so much fun!"

Just as the coffee pot finally quit gurgling, Angie poured herself another cup and asked, "Do you want to go sit in the sun for a while before you get started with your editing?"

"Absolutely, it's a beautiful morning!"

They went outside onto the big back deck, and Angie sat in one of the chairs facing the sun. She closed her eyes and leaned back in her chair, her flowing blonde hair glowing in the light of the morning sunshine. Caleb gazed at her beauty for a few moments before closing his own eyes to soak up the warmth. He marveled at how she could be so feminine, and yet so strong at the same time.

Eventually they were jolted out of their rest by the her phone jingle. She picked it up and Caleb could hear a woman's voice on the other end of the call. Angie finished the call saying, "Okay, I'll get ready and meet you at the book store coffee shop on County Line at 11:00."

Caleb asked, "Was that Jessie?"

"It was. We are going to meet at the book store for coffee, and to talk over our plans."

"Sounds good. Let me get you a model release for her to sign. Might as well get that over with."

Angie arose and went into the bathroom while Caleb walked in and powered up his old desktop computer. As he read through the final chapter of his book, his thoughts drifted to to the series of events that had led to this point. A lump formed in his throat as he thought back on the death of the beloved Yellowstone wolf Luna and subsequent publishing of his book *Spirit of the Wolf*, written in her honor to raise awareness of the wolf slaughter in western America. He thought of the love of his youth Lacey, and her sudden and unexpected passing from cancer. He marveled at the sequence of events that had reunited him with his first friend in Montana, at her suggestion that he get involved with the battle to save the Sand Wash Basin wild horse herd in western Colorado. He wondered about an Unseen Hand guiding his steps. He thought to himself, "*Surely all of this could not have happened by simple chance?*"

"Okay Caleb, I'm out the door. Good luck with your editing!"

"Have fun with Jessica. I hope you make some good progress! If you think of a name for your business, maybe you can go downtown and get a business license and a trade name."

"Maybe... Well, I'll see you later."

"Later!" replied Caleb.

Just as she was pulling into the parking lot Angie got a text from Jessica, "I'm already inside, so come on in when you get here."

Angie parked her car and texted back, "I'm here, be there in a sec."

Angie and Jessica hugged and sat down. Angie handed her the model release and said, “Caleb said he was fine with doing some photo sessions with us. He just wants you to sign the model release so he can use the pictures in his business too.”

“Okay, no problem. That's awesome he's going to help us!”

Angie said, “Let's leave our stuff on the table and go order some coffee. I had a couple cups at home, but after last night I'm definitely going to need some more!”

“Yeah, I woke up a bit groggy myself.”

“Caleb thinks we should start our own line of clothing. That's what his ex did before she passed away.”

“Wow, I didn't know. That's really sad.”

“Yeah, he met her in college out in California. She was going to fashion school while he was taking photography. She hit it pretty big in modeling and her agency sent her out to New York, and then to London. I guess that's when she got her idea for starting a clothing line. The modeling lifestyle got to her and she wanted something a little more stable. Plus I think she missed Caleb and wanted to be where he was.”

“What kind of clothing did she design?”

“Well it was Montana, so I guess she was kind of limited to outdoorsy stuff, fashionable hiking and mountain climbing lines. And I think she also sold a lot of casual wear.”

Jessica replied, “Well, this is Colorado and sportswear is big business here too.”

"Yeah, we could have a line for all seasons. We have the snow skiing in the winter, and with all the reservoirs we could have an entirely different line of summer workout and beach wear."

"But how do we get started?"

"I'm not exactly sure, but Caleb said to start by finding suppliers and manufacturers. I guess we could make some of our own and find suppliers for the rest. Caleb said he could design us a logo that we could start using right away. I guess the first thing we need to do is brainstorm a business name!"

"How about Sportswear by Jessie and Angie?"

Angie laughed, "Well... that sounds like an excellent place to start anyway! By the way, Caleb wants to know if we might want to go with him out to western Colorado to do a western style shoot with the Sand Wash Basin wild mustangs. We'll have to rough camp part of the time, but he also thought maybe we could spend a night in Steamboat and do a high fashion shoot out in the streets."

"Oh, that sounds like a blast! When do we go?"

"Probably right away, he's about ready to publish his book about the horses and wants to get out to check on them. The last time we saw them they were in the middle of a roundup. We think Winter Storm had already passed away, and they had his son Swift Thunder in the chute to be taken away. But he jumped out before they could get him in the pen, so we are hoping he will be able to start a band of his own and carry on Storm's lineage."

"Awesome, I'll round up my camping stuff. I'm ready to go any time you are!"

"Okay I'll tell Caleb, he'll be excited to go right away. You know... he didn't think you would want to go. He thinks you are girly."

Jessica laughed, "Well I guess I'll have to show him a thing or two. This is horse country down here, and I grew up in the dirt!"

"There are ranches and horses all over the place down here, but you kind of forget that we are nothing like the city people up in Denver!"

The two women sipped coffee and talked over their ideas while doing whatever research they could get done on their phones. Eventually the two parted ways with Angie saying, "Okay, have a great day Jessie! I'll let Caleb know to make the plans for the trip out west!"

"I can't wait... see you later then!"

Road Trip to the Sand Wash Basin

Soon the day of the trip to the Sand Wash Basin and Steamboat Springs was at hand, with the trio rolling down the highway in Angie's SUV and Caleb at the wheel. They had long since left the city behind, and were speeding down the big descent into Idaho Springs.

Jessica asked, "Should we stop in Idaho Springs and get something to eat?"

Caleb replied, "I am boycotting Idaho Springs."

"Why?" asked Jessica.

"They have a racket going there. I came up here to photograph Oktoberfest one time and there was nowhere to park in the lot, so I parked on one of the side streets. There was clearly a curb where I stopped, and I was careful not to block anyone's driveway. When I was ready to leave, I went back and my truck was gone. I called the police to report the theft, and they already knew all about it. Some homeowner had called the police and said I was blocking their driveway, so the police had it towed it to an impound lot. Apparently the rednecks in Idaho Springs like to park their trucks in their front yards, and the police have a racket going with the tow truck company to make money towing visitor's cars."

Jessica exclaimed, "Damn, were you able to get your truck back?"

"It wasn't easy. The tow truck company charged a huge hookup fee, and then wouldn't take a credit card for payment. I didn't have the cash on me to pay the fee, so I walked down to the grocery store to beg them to cash a check. The store manager took pity and cashed a check, but he was pissed at the city because apparently I was just the next in a long line of people who had come there to get cash."

Angie said, "Doesn't it seem kind of counterproductive to hold an event where you hope to bring in visitors to your town, and then scam them so that they never come back?"

Caleb answered, "I guess they figure most people will never find out, and a few upset people won't affect overall attendance. But for me, Idaho Springs is never going to get another dime of my money."

Angie replied, "I don't blame you."

Caleb asked, "How about Cajun food for lunch?"

Jessica answered first, "I love Cajun food!"

"Me too!" Angie chimed in.

"Well there's a nice Cajun place in Winter Park., so we'll stop there if it's okay with you two."

"Works for me!" replied Angie.

"Me too, I can't wait!"

Idaho Springs was soon in the rear view mirror, and soon Caleb made the turn onto Highway 40 over Berthoud Pass into the mountains.

As they near the summit Jessica exclaimed, "Wow, this scenery is amazing!"

"You've never been up here?" Caleb asked.

"It's been a long time I guess, I don't think I remember it."

Angie asked, "You don't ever come up to Winter Park to ski?"

"No, I'm not into skiing."

"Yeah, I'm not either."

"Me either." added Caleb. "I'd rather go snowshoeing, no crowds and a lot less hassle. I can snowshoe right out of the back door if we have enough snow. If we don't, Conifer is as far as I have to go to find a snowshoe trail."

Soon the trio was seated at a table looking at a menu.

Caleb said, "I always get the blackened catfish. I should probably try something else, but once I find something I like I tend to stick with it. Oh... and if you order a beer it will come in a mason jar, which for some reason I find kind of cool. Maybe I'm part Cajun."

Angie laughed and replied, "I don't know of any blond Cajuns. I think you are just channeling your inner redneck."

Caleb laughed, "Maybe so."

They finished their meals, and were soon back on the road.

Caleb said, "I was planning to make it all the way to the Sand Wash today, but it's getting kind of late so maybe we should stop in Steamboat for the night. We can book a room there."

Jessica said, "I don't know if I can afford a room."

“We can get a double,” replied Angie. “Just pitch in whatever you can. Besides, Caleb is saving money by not having to pay models for his photoshoot, right Caleb?”

Caleb laughed, “I guess that's one way to look at it.”

“Okay cool! Thanks you guys.”

The trio rolled into Steamboat late in the afternoon and quickly found a hotel with vacancy. Caleb asked, “How about this one, it looks like it has a lounge for us to relax and have a drink later?”

Angie replied, “Looks good to me!”

Jessica chimed in as well, “I'm just along for the ride!”

Caleb got out his credit card and walked to the front desk to check on a room.

“How many will be staying tonight?” the receptionist inquired.

“We have three, would it be possible to get a double room with two beds?”

“That will be fine sir, it's the off season and we have plenty of rooms.”

Caleb made the payment and then walked back to the soft chairs where Angie and Jessica were resting. “We are all checked in, so I guess we might as well get settled. I'll bring the vehicle around front so we can unload.”

The team was traveling light, so it only took a few minutes to get settled into the room.

Angie asked, "Should we go to the bar and get a drink?"

Caleb replied, "That sounds good, but we still have a little light left. Should we go out and and do a little fashion session first?"

Angie answered, "I guess I'm up for a short session, how about you Jessie?"

"I'm game," she replied.

"Okay, why don't you two get dressed and I'll go out and gather some lighting equipment."

Caleb was dialing in his lighting gear when Angie and Jessica appeared, wearing sundresses and broad brimmed sun hats. Caleb snapped a few pictures as Angie twirled and posed. Jessica followed close behind with a twirl and a sexy pose with one hand on the brim of her hat. Caleb checked his exposures on the back of the camera, made a slight adjustment and motioned toward some shops down the street.

"Lets walk down to the shops and use the show windows as a backdrop for a few pictures."

The two models sashayed out ahead, while Caleb kept his camera trained on the women. He watched carefully for their nods and glances, the little signals that they were prepared for an image capture. At one point, in unspoken agreement they whirled around and posed together, arms around each other with their heads slightly tilted inward.

"That's great!" commented Caleb. "That's going to be a great cover shot for your website...when I get it built for you that is."

And so they continued down the street, laughing and posing and talking excitedly about their new business venture.

Eventually the warm Colorado sun dipped below the horizon, and Caleb adjusted his camera to capture the warm tungsten lights of the shop windows. After a few more poses, the late autumn temperature began to drop precipitously, and Caleb heard Jessica exclaim, "Brrr!"

Caleb caught the cue and commented, "It is getting chilly, should we head for the lounge for a drink?"

Angie replied, "Definitely yes, these sundresses aren't made for a fall evening in Colorado!"

Jessica asked Caleb, "Is there a way you can get these pictures downloaded to our phones? I want to get some of these on my Instapix tonight!"

"Sure, why don't you two order us some drinks, and I'll go out and get my laptop. I can transfer the pictures to your phones from there."

Angie and Jessica were each sipping a glass of white wine when Caleb returned with his laptop. He noticed a bottle of microbrew and a full glass at his seat, and Angie said "We thought you would probably want a beer."

"You know me well!" replied Caleb.

Caleb booted up his laptop as the two women excitedly discussed their website.

Angie asked, "Caleb, can you throw us together a front page for our website tonight?"

"Sure, I just need to know what you want the title to be."

Jessica exclaimed, "This is going to be so much fun!"

Caleb soon had the pictures transferred to the soon to be famous Instapix model's phones, and the conversation quickly died down as the pair concentrated on uploading pictures to their respective accounts. With a few pictures uploaded to their nascent business pages and a couple of glasses of wine splashed down, the group was ready to get some sleep.

Jessica exclaimed, "Wow... I'm tired, should we get some rest?"

Angie replied, "Yes, tomorrow is going to be a long day in the sun."

Caleb powered down his laptop and the trio headed up to their room.

Discovery in the Sand Wash

Angie was the first to awaken, and quietly slipped out of the room in the dark to go to the lobby for the complimentary continental breakfast and coffee. The hostess saw her struggling to load up with pastries and three cups of coffee, and offered to help, "Do you need a platter to carry all that up to your room?"

"Oh, that would be amazing!"

Soon Angie slipped back into the room with all the goods, and was greeted by Jessica who was sitting at the little round table in the soft glow of a small lamp, wearing just her sheer nightie.

Angie whispered, "What are you doing in your underwear! What if Caleb wakes up?"

"What, why? He has seen me in lingerie plenty of times shooting our shows, and he will again now that we are in business."

"Well, that's a good point but it seems different here in the hotel room. Wait, are we going to sell lingerie in our shop?" Angie wondered out loud.

"I don't know." replied Jessica. "I don't see why not!"

"I guess we just need to find a supplier. We could make a sales room in our online shop for it."

Soon Caleb was stirring and Jessica threw a long sweatshirt over her nightie. Caleb struggled to open his eyes and stumbled over to the table to join the women.

"So what are we talking about so early this morning?" he asked.

Angie answered, "Oh, we are just discussing whether we want to include lingerie in our shop."

"Well, I don't know why not. Inventory is inventory, and sales are sales."

Jessica replied, "Well, when you put it that way."

"Oh, you have coffee!" exclaimed Caleb.

"Yup, and we have cream and sugar if you want."

Angie laughed and said, "Caleb likes his coffee black. Not only that, but you are probably about to hear his story about his favorite little barista that said "He likes his medicine straight!""

"Well I'm not going to tell it now, you already gave up the punch line!"

Angie smiled, "I know, I've heard it a hundred times."

Caleb responded, "Well maybe not a hundred."

Angie asked, "Are we in a hurry to get to the Sand Wash today?"

Caleb answered, "Not a big hurry I guess. We just need to get there in time to make it to get up to the north side in time to check on the horses and do a late afternoon photoshoot while the light is still nice."

"So leave here by lunch time? Jessie and I want to go downtown and look at clothes."

“That should work, checkout isn't until 11:00. That will give me time to get out my laptop and work on yesterday's pictures. Maybe I can get some of them posted before we head out.”

Jessica asked, “Can you put some more of them on our phones while you are at it?”

“Sure, just make sure you are back around 10:00 so I have time before we check out.”

Caleb didn't notice that 10:00 had come and gone, as he worked diligently on the previous day's pictures. Finally at about 10:45, the two women knocked on the door and Caleb got up from his chair to let them in. He was surprised to see a variety of bags and boxes, almost too much for them to carry.

With a big smile Angie said, “ We found a few things for our photoshoot later today!”

Caleb laughed, “I see that! Hey I have some pictures ready to save on your phones, and then we'd better hit the road.”

Jessica exclaimed, “I can't wait to see them!”

“Can we get some lunch before we leave town? I'm hungry.”

Caleb replied, “I don't see why not, I guess we aren't on any kind of hard schedule. Why don't you two get packed up while I download the pictures to your phones. Then maybe you can look the brochures over for a nice lunch place while I lug our stuff out to the car.”

Filled with anticipation and a good lunch, the trio was soon rolling west on Highway 40 toward Craig. Caleb's mind was focused on the welfare of the wild mustangs and what images he might be able to capture, while the two models were still discussing their own agenda.

Jessica asked, “Caleb, do you think you could do a launch story for us with links to our Instapix accounts?”

“I'm sure that would be no problem. Perhaps we can find a hill to set up camp, somewhere there is a phone signal where I can set up the laptop and work on it.”

“That would be awesome Caleb!” added Angie.

Jessica exclaimed, “Angie, look at this one of us together! We should use this as a banner for our Facetime page!”

“Oh, that's a good one! Caleb, you did such a nice job on these!”

“Thank you Angie, I'm sure I'll have many more for you soon! Hey, there's a Shopmart in Craig. Do we need to stop for any more supplies, or use the restroom before we head into no man's land?”

“That would probably be a good idea,” replied Angie. “Maybe we should pick up a couple of umbrellas for shade, and for props in the pictures.”

“That's a great idea,” replied Caleb. “The hot Colorado afternoon sun can get pretty harsh for portrait lighting.”

Soon the trio was finished in Craig and on their way west to the Sand Wash Basin.

“Where's the turnoff for the Sand Wash Caleb?” asked Angie.

"We're looking for the town of Maybell. We will turn off of 40 there and head northwest on 318 past Sunbeam and into the countryside."

"Okay, I'll GPS it while we still have a signal."

Jessica added, "Wow, this is some seriously desolate terrain. I don't see how horses can even live here."

"There are a few watering holes, but it's a pretty harsh existence. It doesn't help that the BLM allows sheep herders to turn their livestock loose in the horse management area."

Angie exclaimed with great excitement, "Caleb, we are almost there! It's only a quarter of an inch on my phone. How far is that?"

Caleb laughed, "I don't know, but I think we are less than 20 minutes to the turn."

Eventually the sign for the Sand Wash came into view, and Caleb turned into the refuge.

Jessica spotted a big welcome sign and said, "There's an information sign, should we go look at it?"

Caleb replied, "I don't think we need to, unless you really want to see it."

"No I'm good. How much further to see the horses?"

"We could see a few at any time now, but I imagine the main herd is up on the northeast side. It's probably another couple of hours up to there, but we'll stop and take a break at about 3:00 to shoot pictures."

"Okay, cool."

Angie exclaimed, "Caleb look, a couple of mustangs just ahead!"

"Good eye, it looks like they are on a mission. Maybe there's a watering hole near here."

Caleb slowly negotiated the rough dirt road, dodging rocks and holes and looking for a good location for a photoshoot. Eventually the sun made it's way across the blazing blue Colorado sky, and shadows began to form on the east side of rocks and bluffs.

Angie was scanning the landscape ahead of them, when she saw something unusual, "What's that, it looks like some kind of corral or something?"

Caleb replied, "I wonder if that's the live bait trap?"

"What's that?" asked Jessica.

"Well I guess they finally got enough public pressure to end the helicopter round ups, so now they are just trapping a few at a time by putting food and water inside a locking corral."

"That's just mean."

"I agree, and a lot of other people think so too. Let's go up there and see what's going on."

As they drew closer Angie asked, "Is that Stormy?"

Caleb answered, "I don't know, it's been so long since we've seen him."

Jessica chimed in, “Look, there's nobody around. What if the food runs out, or if one of them gets hurt?”

“That's the BLM for you. They talk a big story, but in the end they really don't give a crap about the welfare of the horses. Now if it was the ranchers and their stupid sheep, you can believe they'd be right on it.”

Angie exclaimed, “Hey, there's a dust cloud approaching from the south. What if it's the government, we'd better get going!”

Caleb replied, “I have half a notion to come back in the dark and turn them loose. Take the wheel, I'm going to set a way point on my GPS trail tracker.”

“I've got it.”

“Okay, way point set. Let's go on ahead a mile or two and set up camp. I might sneak back in when it gets dark and open the gate.”

Angie exclaimed, “Caleb, seriously?”

“Well, we got away with it last time.”

“I suppose we did didn't we.”

Caleb continued driving north until he spotted a faint path leading off to the west, to a rocky bluff a quarter mile off the main road.

“That looks like a good place to do a photoshoot, doesn't it?”

Angie replied, “Yeah, we can pose on those rocks and you can see the Bear Ears in the background. It looks perfect!”

"Plus we will be off the main road in case the feds drive out this way."

Caleb turned his four wheel drive of the main road and pulled back behind the bluff, and out of sight of the main road. Angie and Jessica began shuffling through their new packages as Caleb parked the vehicle. Caleb went around to the rear and opened the hatch to retrieve his photography gear, including his camera and a couple of battery powered off camera strobes.

He was about to suggest emptying out the back in order to make a dressing room, when he noticed Jessica already out of her top and halfway into another one.

"Jeez Jessie, you are almost naked!"

"So what, there's nobody out here to see us!"

"Well Caleb..." she started to say. "Oh never mind," she laughed. "I guess this whole place is our dressing room today."

Caleb set up his key and fill lights, and pointed towards the rocks, "I have the lights set up for this area here. As long as you pose in the general area we should have good exposures."

Angie went first, wearing a red leather skirt with a matching fringed vest.

"That's pretty cool," commented Caleb. "Did you get that today?"

"Yeah, we got some really fun western wear in town."

Jessica was next, also sporting a fringed vest with matching hat and leather boots.

With about two hours of good light behind them, the photoshoot was coming to an end and Caleb commented, “It's getting a little dark, I guess we should probably put up the tent before the bugs get too bad.”

Jessica replied, “This was so much fun, thank you Caleb!”

“You are certainly welcome, you two are a blast to photograph. I can't wait for your little business to take off!”

Soon the tent was erected and air mattresses inflated. Caleb set up the battery unit inside the tent, and hooked up a couple power cables.

“You two can both recharge your phones at the same time. I'm going to quick copy today's pictures to your phones so you can have something to do tonight when I go over to the holding corral.”

Jessica responded, “You are going to walk over there in the dark, won't you get lost?”

“No worries, I'll have my GPS and a fully charged LED flashlight. I'll set a way point for this location, and I've already got one for the corral. The worst I should have to worry about is a coyote or two, and they aren't going to bother me.”

“Are you sure Caleb?” asked Angie. “This seems like a dumb idea.”

Caleb laughed, “I've done much dumber things than this.”

Angie couldn't mask the worry in her voice when she said, “I suppose. You were always getting in trouble in Montana. If I remember right, we even had to bail you out of jail.”

"Yeah, and I'd break that trap again if I had the chance."

"I know, it was the right thing to do."

Caleb put on his thermal hiking gear, and a black hat to hide his blond hair. With water bottles in the side pouches, some snacks and a bolt cutter in his pack and trail tracker in hand, Caleb slipped away into the darkness.

Angie yelled after him, "When will you be back?"

"A couple hours, maybe three or four."

"Good luck!" exclaimed Jessica.

"Thanks, don't worry!"

Jessica asked worriedly, "Is he going to be alright?"

"Knowing Caleb he will be just fine. A few years ago up in Montana some hunters ambushed him from behind and took him out into the snow with nothing, and left him for dead."

"Seriously, how did he survive?"

"Well had had his survival knife with matches in the handle. He managed to make a fire to survive the night. When it got light in the morning he figured out where he was and hiked out."

"Wow, that's amazing! I hope he has his knife with him tonight."

"I'm sure he does. It also has a compass in case his trail tracker fails."

"Well, should we get to work posting our pictures?" asked Jessica.

"Might as well, I'm not going to be able to get any sleep with him out there in the dark."

Daring Rescue

A sliver of the waning Harvest Moon provided a faint ghostly glow on the desolate landscape of the Sand Wash Basin, as Caleb strode through the cold Colorado night. He shivered a bit as he zipped up his old military field jacket that he had brought home to California from the war years before. He was suddenly aware that he was as a speck of dust in the vast emptiness of the western Rockies, and he reached behind for assurance that he was accompanied by his trusty knife that he affectionately called JC. Someone asked him one time why the name JC, and his brief reply was simply, "Just in Case."

As he looked around he was struck by the fact that there wasn't a trace of man made light to spoil the view of the vast canopy of stars overhead. It wasn't difficult to imagine how the Milky Way received it's name. Billions of stars appearing so dense in the sky that it seemed like someone had splashed a glass of milk from horizon to horizon. Soon his thoughts turned to Angie and Jessie waiting for him in the tent, and he quickened his pace. As he fixed his gaze on the trail before him, a pair of glowing yellow eyes accompanied by a low growl stopped him in his tracks. He wondered, "*Was a bear blocking his path, or maybe a wolf or a mountain lion*?" He knew it was most likely just a coyote, but he was taking no chances and avoided the animal by veering off the beaten path with a more direct approach to the corral.

As he strode through the darkness, he pulled out his flashlight for a quick look behind to see if the critter was stalking him. Seeing no sign of the predator, he exchanged his flashlight for the GPS trail tracker unit. Muscle memory guided his finger to the power button, and he activated the device. He stopped and watched the display come to life as a satellite was acquired, and his path ahead illuminated. He clicked the zoom button a few times until the way points for the corral ahead, and campsite behind were clearly defined. A wave of relief flowed over him as he realized he was heading directly for the corral, with a bright line clearly pointing the way back to the campsite.

With renewed confidence, Caleb charged ahead on his way to the mustang corral. With less than a quarter mile to go according to the trail tracker, he found himself at the base of a steep hill. Undaunted, he moved carefully ahead hoping there were no unexpected ledges or impassable cliffs to block his progress. He felt safe hiking on the plateau with no flashlight, but now he felt a bit of LED illumination would be a better choice. Slowly he made his way up the hill, looking forward to the moment when he would see the magnificent wild horses charging out of the corral and running free once again.

Caleb stopped in his tracks as he neared the top of the hill. He had been worried that the feds would appear while he was at the corral, but was surprised to hear voices just the same. He crouched to the ground and moved in closer behind a large boulder where he could try to identify the men.

Upon closer inspection, he could see two bearded men sitting at a campfire. They were passing a bottle back and forth, which Caleb guessed was filled with hard liquor. From the sound of their boisterous voices, he also surmised that they were becoming quite drunk. "*But what are they doing here*?" he wondered. "*They obviously aren't feds.*"

Caleb heard one of the men say, "Tell me again, who's coming to pick up these horses?"

"We have a deal to sell them directly to some south of border rancheros."

"What about the BLM, aren't they supposed to auction them off here in the states?"

"So what, how are they going to know if a few horses are missing. It's not like they are branded or anything."

"What do some Mexican ranchers want with a bunch of wild horses?"

"I don't think they really want them. They sell them to the slaughter houses by the pound, almost pure profit. All they have to do is send some hands to come and get them. We all make money and these vermin aren't eating our grass anymore," the first man bellowed.

"Well how much longer do we have to sit here?"

"I don't know, they said they'd be here by midnight."

Caleb looked at his watch and realized he was probably running out of time. He figured the men were so drunk they wouldn't notice him sneaking behind the corral, but he thought he'd let them finish their bottle anyway. "*Maybe they will just pass out*," he thought to himself. Soon the conversation began to ebb, and he heard the bottle hit the ground. He took that as his cue to sneak behind the corral and open the gate. Unfortunately though, the gate was locked with a chain and a padlock. There was a heavy bolt cutter in his pack but this was a big lock. He hoped it would be able to penetrate the heavy steel without too much effort.

Horses nickered as he worked, but the two men remained fast asleep. The lock proved to be too much for the cutter, so Caleb switched to cutting the chain. The steel chain was also formidable, but wasn't made of the same hardened steel as the lock. Now all that was needed was to pull the broken chain out of the fence, and he worked it through as quietly as possible. However the mustangs were starting to get excited, nickering more frequently and stomping at the hard ground. "*Please don't wake them up*," Caleb thought to himself.

Soon the gate was open and the horses were stampeding to freedom. Caleb stood at the gate and watched as the herd galloped past. The quiet of the night was shattered as the animals banged into metal posts, in their frantic dash for freedom. Suddenly he heard one of the men holler, "Hey, what's going on, who's there?"

As the last couple of horses burst through the gate, Caleb made a run for it toward the west. One of the men scrambled to get his powerful flashlight, but by then Caleb was well out of range of the beam. He stopped to listen and try to figure out what the men were going to do. "*Will they run for their pickup truck or will they chase me out into the sandy terrain*?" wondered Caleb.

"Did you see somebody?" one man said to the other.

"I think so, I think he took off toward the west."

"Okay, you go after him and I'll circle around to the north and come up from behind."

"What are we going to do if we catch him?"

"I don't know, if he struggles shoot him."

"With pleasure," the other man shouted.

Caleb was well aware the men were drunk and would be unlikely to catch him, but he also didn't want to give them a chance to get back to their truck and possibly find Angie and Jessie camped up the road. He circled around to the south and back toward the corral. When he reached the camp he ran to the pickup and checked the door. As he suspected, the door was unlocked and the window open. Caleb opened the door and reached down to release the hood latch. He scrambled around front to open the hood, and quickly yanked the coil wire from the distributor cap. He didn't want to take the chance of the men catching him and recovering the wire, so he heaved it as far as he could across the road toward the east, and into some thick bramble.

By then one of the men was already returning, bellowing obscenities all the while. When he saw Caleb he yelled, "Son of a bitch, get away from that truck. I'm going to kick your ass!"

Caleb slipped behind the truck and waited to see which way the sheep herder was going to go. When the bearded drunk made his move, Caleb circled around the truck the other way. Just as the man turned around to confront him, Caleb sprayed him straight in the face with bear spray. He knocked the incapacitated man to the ground and delivered a devastating kick to the side of his head. The stunned man lay on the ground groaning as Caleb yanked off his boots, and threw them across the road into the darkness as well.

The other sheepherder was soon approaching as well, "Did you get him?" he hollared. "Are you okay, are you there?"

Of course the downed man was unable to answer, and soon his drunken partner approached the truck breathing like a freight train. Caleb hoped he would keel over from a heart attack before he had to deal with the big bearded sheep herder, but it was not to be. Caleb readied his bear spray, and when the man ran around the truck Caleb blasted him right in the eyes with the wicked mix. The fat man ran in circles cursing and yelling and threatening Caleb, "I'm going to kill you!"

He had no idea Caleb was standing right in front of him, ready with a throat punch that left the drunken fool bent over and gasping for air. Another kick to the the head, and the second man was down as well.

Caleb quickly disposed of his boots and spotted a cell phone attached to his belt, which also went the way of coil wire and boots. He made a quick check for the first rustler's phone and gave it a long toss as well. By the time the two would be horse rustlers regained conciousness, Caleb would be long gone.

Caleb once again reached for his GPS unit, oriented himself and began jogging toward the way point indicating the campsite. About thirty minutes down the hill he burst into the campsite yelling, "Pack up girls, we gotta get going!"

Angie stuck her head out of the tent rubbing her eyes, and said "Caleb, what are you talking about, it's the middle of the night!"

"I know, but I ran into some trouble at the corral, and we have to get going."

"Going, go where?"

"Anywhere but here. Wake up Jessie and let's just throw everything into the hatch. We can sort it out later."

Angie yelled, "Jessie, wake up, we have to get going!"

"What, seriously?"

"Yes, right now. Caleb says there was trouble at the corral and we need to get out of here."

"I need to get dressed."

"No, there's no time for that. Just throw on a t-shirt, you can get dressed in the car on the way."

"On the way where?" Jessica asked as she emerged from the tent, while struggling to get into a long t-shirt."

Soon the trio was packed and on the road and Angie asked, "Where are we going to go?"

Caleb handed Angie the GPS and said, "Let's go out the northeast side of the Wash. We can get on Highway 7 and head back to Steamboat for the night."

He showed Angie how to work the trail tracker and said, "Find us a road heading east."

"Okay, which way is east?"

Caleb pointed to the right and Angie said, "I think there is one coming up. It's about a quarter of an inch, how far is that?"

"I don't know, probably not far. Just keep an eye on the moving dot and let me know when we start to get really close to the turnoff."

A voice came from the backseat, "Shit, I need to get some pants on!"

Angie laughed and said, "Now all of a sudden you are all shy?"

"Well... I just feel stupid back here with no pants on."

Angie handed her a jacket and said, "When we get turned east, I'll go dig around in the back and see if I can find you something."

"Okay."

"Caleb slow down, the turn off is coming right up just ahead."

Caleb made the turn onto a fairly wide dirt road, and it looked like they were home free with only a few miles of wash board surface before reaching the paved surface of Highway 7.

As they cruised through the night Angie asked, "So what happened back there?"

"When I got to the corral there were a couple of sheepherders camped out and drinking hard. They were talking about selling the horses out from under the feds, and said there were some Mexican ranchers coming with a truck tonight to haul the animals over the border for sale to a slaugter house."

Jessica asked, "What did you do?"

"I just waited for them to pass out, and then I cut the chain on the gate and let the horses go. I'm pretty sure I saw Swift Thunder in the group."

"Well didn't they chase you?"

"They did, but I got them with bear spray. I stole the coil wire from their truck and took their shoes, so it will be a while before they will be getting out of there."

"They let you take their shoes?"

Caleb laughed and said, "They weren't in any mood to argue with me at the time."

"Did they see you?" asked Angie.

"I don't think so. Once I got them with the bear spay they

struggled a bit, but before the bear spray wore off they were back to their nap."

"They just fell asleep?"

"Sort of," chuckled Caleb.

Angie looked down at the GPS unit and commented, "We are getting close to Highway 7, so get ready to turn."

"Okay."

Soon the intersection became visible in the glow of the headlights, and he slowed to make the turn. Angie climbed into the back seat to look for some clothes for Jessica, and Caleb settlied in for the long strretch of dark highway into Craig.

"We'll need to stop for gas in Craig. I guess we could look for a motel there, or we could keep going on to Steamboat."

Angie replied, "I'm really tired, maybe we should just stop there and get some sleep. It's already the middle of the night, and it's not like we need anything other than a bed to sleep in."

Jessica added her opinion, "I'm for stopping in Craig."

"Craig it is then!"

Soon Caleb could tell by their breathing that both Angie and Jessica were sound asleep. He would probably be sleepy as well, were it not for the adrenyline still pumping through his system from the confrontation earlier. He opened the driver side window to let in some cool fresh air, and set the cruise control for a safe speed just below the speed limit.

Terror in the Sky

Ember and Shadow were blissfully unaware of the plight of Colorado's wild horse population. The young wolves were enjoying their new lives together, and filled with joy at finding a life long partner They had moved several miles from Ember's natal pack, and were busy marking a home range for themselves in the rugged Oregon wilderness. They would most likely have pups to raise the next spring, and would need space to hunt for sustenance and room to train their young to be important assets for a future pack

Their new life together was not without peril though. The small parcel of land was part of the territory formerly claimed by Ember's natal pack, and numerous encounters with her siblings required careful diplomacy. On the other side of their domain lurked hostile packs continually seeking an advantage for themselves. Fortunately for the time being, the outside packs were unaware of the new arrangement in the Aspen Butte family and continued to respect old boundaries, largely leaving the new mates alone.

Without a mature pack to assist them, Ember and Shadow were content to avoid larger prey. There were plenty of small animals in their territory, and the pair spent their days leisurely snatching prey from their grassy hiding places. This day was like any other, and the mates had full bellies from a successful day of rabbit hunting. The nights were getting colder though and on this chilly evening, Ember busied herself digging a shallow bed under a rock outcropping where they could snuggle and keep warm and dry until the warm sunshine began to penetrate the pine canopy in the morning.

When the bed was ready, Ember approached Shadow and licked his face affectionately. She did not resist his loving kisses in return, and beckoned for him to join her in their temporary den. Their winter coats were already coming in to keep them warm, and the couple quickly drifted off to sleep to the eerie howls of the Aspen Butte Pack in the distance.

As the first rays of light streamed into their den, Shadow was awakened by a strange sound. It was a noise he had never heard before, and it was growing louder by the second. He perked up his ears in curiosity, and trotted out into a clearing to investigate the possible threat. Eventually the deafening roar was directly overhead, forcing the young wolf into terrified flight. The black monster followed his every move from above, and he was unable to outrun the beast. Eventually exhausted and realizing it was impossible to escape, he courageously turned to fight. With a blast from the untouchable foe overhead, Shadow suddenly found himself trapped inside the clutches of an enemy he had never experienced in his brief lifetime.

An equally traumatized Ember chased her mate and desperately bit at the ropes that had entrapped him. Soon another loud boom sounded and Ember also found herself entangled in another weapon launched by the rumbling predator overhead. Soon a pack of two legged intruders burst out of the forest and approached the terrified animals. Ember watched in fear as her mate suddenly lay motionless on the ground. She felt a sharp sting and soon her world also blurred and went black.

A groggy Ember slowly regained consciousness, only to become aware of the steel jaws of a tiny prison preventing her escape to the wilderness, and only home she had ever known. A muffled woof drew her attention and she discovered her beloved mate in a similar steel prison next to her. The cages had been placed close enough for the two wolves to touch each other, and Shadow licked her face incessantly as he attempted to fully revive her.

There was no light in their dungeon, only an unfamiliar deafening and unrelenting roar that was intolerable to their sensitive ears.. With nothing but each other to provide consolation, the two remained in close contact throughout their journey to a new land. They were unaware of their destination, but were unknowingly on their way to the mountains of Colorado as part of an experiment to reintroduce wolves to that state following their extinction in the previous century.

Ember's ears perked up at a change in pitch in the terrible noise that continued to punish their aching eardrums. Both animals leaped to their feet as a violent shaking invaded their new dark world. Suddenly both wolves lost their balance as a unseen force propelled them to the front of their cages. As they regained their feet, their world stopped moving and the terrible noise finally subsided. Then there was complete silence for a moment before light streamed in from above. Strange voices accompanied the two legged predators that had confronted them in the forest, and their cages lurched violently upward. Shadow howled in dismay as his mate disappeared through the point of light in their dark sky.

He lost his balance as his cage also careened upward toward the point of light in the sky, and he cried in terror at the unknown scene that appeared before him. A familiar scent soon comforted him and regained his balance as he cage was rolled forward. Finally he was once again reunited with his mate who yipped with joy at the sight of him.

Ember sensed a welcome change in the hospitality of their new unfamiliar and cruel world, as the two cages were handed off to a new set of two legged caretakers. A kind voice spoke softly to them in a language they did not comprehend, but understood to be gentle and caring. Ember began to understand that their two legged benefactors were not going to harm them, and turned to lick the face of her distressed partner.

Suddenly their cages jolted upward again and they were thrust back into darkness. The ground beneath them began once again to jostle their cages, but this time they were spared the terrifying din of jet engines.

Ember and Shadow squeezed together as closely as possible for what little warmth was available to them. They eventually grew accustomed to the constant growl of the truck's diesel engine, and fell asleep in the comfort of each other's presence.

Finally the big door flew open and the light of a full moon spilled into the back of the truck. Once again the humans appeared, and their cages were gently lifted down and placed together on rollers. Ember waited with quiet optimism, but Shadow lunged and snapped his jaws at his unwelcome captors.. Once again, Ember watched as her mate yelped and suddenly lay down as though dead. She too felt the painful sting of a tranquilizer dart and joined her mate in deep sleep.

Shadow was the first to awaken as he took a deep breath of fresh mountain air. For the first time in two days the familiar light of a full moon overhead provided comfort and hope that his terrible ordeal was finally over. Ember began to stir as well and Shadow went to her immediately, once again licking her face to give her confidence that she was safe in the presence of her powerful mate.

Once fully awake, the pair explored the perimeter of their new domain. They were not able to run to freedom as they would have liked, but their new surroundings were much more like the wilderness they were so rudely snatched from two days prior. Ember was the first to discover the shelter that had been provided for them, and went inside to investigate. Shadow followed her inside, and it wasn't long before Colorado's exhausted new residents were snuggled together and sound asleep.

Thanksgiving

Michelle was the first to awaken on Thanksgiving day, and took a deep breath to fill her nostrils with the aroma of a large turkey breast simmering in the crock pot. She noticed that the water in the pot had boiled down a bit overnight, and added a pint before pouring a cup of coffee into her insulated mug. "*Wow, what a gloomy morning,*" she thought to herself as she went to sit down at the kitchen table. As she took her first sip, a quick glance out the big picture window revealed the season's first snowflakes, slowly drifting through the pine trees on the eastern ledge of beautiful Castlewood Canyon State Park. For a second she felt a twinge of loneliness, as she thought of her mom so far away in her home town of Gardiner., Montana. Growing up, most of her Thanksgiving mornings were spent helping her mom get the cafe ready for visitors, and locals without close family to celebrate with.

However the feeling quickly passed as she took in the magical scene outside, and she set her mind on the fun day she had planned with her new family in Colorado. Caleb and Angie weren't actually family, but Caleb had been part of her life for so long that she thought of him as an older brother. She was also grateful to Angie who had taken her in after graduating from college, treating her like a sister when she needed a home.

Soon Caleb entered the room and walked over to the sliding glass doors to take a look out back at the weather. "I didn't know it was supposed to snow today," he commented.

"I didn't either," replied Michelle. "I guess you never know what is going to happen with the weather around here."

"I think I'll put on my jacket and go for a trek with my camera. I love these snowy holidays when I get to have the whole forest to myself, at least for a while anyway. I imagine there will be a pretty good crowd once people get done with their meals, but I'll be back by then. Do you want to come with me?"

Michelle replied, "No, I think I'll just drink some coffee and enjoy the snow from the kitchen table."

Caleb laughed and said, "That's what I figured, but I didn't want to be rude."

Angie was next to enter the room, rubbing her eyes and exclaiming, "Hey, it's snowing! I didn't know that was supposed to happen today."

Michelle laughed, "Well that makes three of us!"

Angie looked into the crock pot and asked, "Did somebody add some water this morning?"

"I did," replied Michelle. "It looked a little low."

"Perfect," replied Angie. "Caleb, aren't you going to sit and have some coffee?"

"Maybe later, you know how I can't resist the snow."

"Of course, I still remember that first Christmas Eve in Montana at the Alpine Tap. You had been out all day with your camera when you finally stopped in for a beer."

"I remember that Christmas well," mused Caleb. "You were just about the first person I met after arriving there!"

"Well have fun then, Michelle and I will be thinking of you by yourself out in the cold."

Caleb grabbed his camera and slipped out the sliding glass doors into the snow, which by now was coming down harder and blowing around furiously.

"Do you need me to do anything?" asked Michelle.

"No thanks, the turkey can simmer a couple more hours before we need to get up and do anything. Let's just sit here and relax."

"Should we see if the parades are on TV yet?"

"Sure, New York is two hours later than Colorado so they will probably be getting started right about now."

Michelle's phone rang just as Angie got up, and she answered it with a cheery "hello!"

"Hi Michelle, this is Heather. Happy Thanksgiving!"

"Happy Thanksgiving to you too! I'm surprised to hear from you this morning, is there a problem over at the park?"

"No, but I wanted to be the first to tell you that we have a date for the wolf release."

"What, seriously? I didn't even know we had wolves yet."

"We've had them for a few weeks now, doing health checks and stuff. But anyway, we are going to be setting them free out in western Colorado in a couple weeks!"

"Oh Heather, that is so exciting! Can I tell Caleb?"

"Yes you can tell him, but he can't say anything yet as the time and location are going to be a secret. We will have a news crew there, but Caleb can do some still images for his own story if he would like to."

"Oh you can bet he will be there! Can Angie come too?"

"Sure, I don't see why not. I'll let you know where and when once we get all the details ironed out, and a final date set."

"I can't wait to tell Caleb, he's going to be so excited!"

Heather laughed and said, "I thought this might brighten up your holiday!"

"It certainly did!"

"Well once again, happy Thanksgiving!"

"You have a wonderful day too, and stay warm!"

"What, what is going on?" asked Angie.

"Oh my God Angie, they are going to be releasing wolves pretty soon. And you and Caleb get to be there too!"

"We'd better make sure Caleb is sitting down when we tell him," laughed Angie.

"Yeah, he might injure himself!"

Angie and Michelle finished their coffee and Angie said, "Well, I suppose we can start getting the sides and desserts going."

"Okay, what do you want me to do?"

Just then Caleb burst through the sliding doors, along with a cloud of swirling snow.

Angie greeted him, "Hey Caleb, did you have a nice hike?"

"I did, it was very peaceful in the falling snow. No other people are in the park yet."

Michelle followed up saying, "Caleb, guess what?"

"What?"

"We have some exciting news!"

"Well lay it on me!" he laughed.

"I got a call from Heather a little bit ago and she says they have wolves available and are almost ready to release them into the wild."

"What, seriously?"

"Yes, they are finishing up on health checks and will be setting a date in December to release them. Guess what else!"

"I can't imagine."

"You and Angie get to go along and be a part of it!"

"Cool... wow!"

"Only you can't write anything yet, and you can't tell anyone either. Heather said there would be a news crew, but you are welcome to shoot stills and write a story about it."

"Awesome, I can't wait! Did we get any champagne for today?"

"No, we'll have to settle for wine," replied Angie.

"Well no matter, it's a great day anyway!"

Eventually Thanksgiving dinner was ready and the three friends sat down together at the table.

"Caleb, do you want to say the grace?"

"Sure."

The trio held hands and bowed their heads as Caleb thanked the Almighty for the good fortune they had been granted over the past few years of tumultuous change in their lives.

Angie began the meal by taking a slice of turkey breast for herself, and handing the bowl and knife to Michelle. Caleb opened a bottle of California white wine and poured three glasses.

"I wonder how the new pack will get along out there in western Colorado. That's some pretty desolate country, certainly not my first choice for their new home," Caleb wondered aloud.

"Yeah, I wonder why they don't put them in the trees somewhere," added Angie.

Michelle replied, "Wolves can travel a very long way in a short time. They will find the trees if they aren't happy out in the high plains."

"I hope they don't go up to Wyoming or out to Utah. Hunters will be waiting for them, just like they do for the Yellowstone wolves at the border of the park," said Angie.

"I don't think the Colorado ranchers out west are going to be too happy with them either. And I don't imagine they care about any laws passed in Denver to protect the new pack. They will shoot them on sight, and it will be war between the Denver environmentalists and the western slope rednecks," commented Caleb.

Michelle replied indignantly, "Well it will be a hundred thousand dollar fine if we catch them. Hopefully that will be enough of a deterrent to keep those hill billies in line."

"I hope so," replied Caleb.

The trio looked at each other in surprise when the doorbell unexpectedly rang.

"Are you expecting anyone?" Caleb asked.

Both Michelle and Angie shrugged their shoulders and shook their heads no.

Caleb arose to answer the door and looked out the peephole.

"It's Jessie!"

"Well let her in Caleb, it's cold out there!" Angie yelled across the room.

Caleb opened the door and invited Jessica in, asking "What are you doing out in the snow?"

"My husband has a bunch of his buddies over watching football, and they all seem to think I'm their personal waitress. I thought it might be more fun to hang out with you guys!"

Angie laughed, "I don't know how much fun we're having, but we are having a nice relaxing afternoon!. Have you eaten?"

"Yes, we ate and then all his friends invaded our living room."

"Would you like a glass of wine, or a cup of coffee or something?"

"Sure, a glass of wine would be nice."

"Well, why don't you have a seat in the living room. We are just getting ready to watch some holiday movies on the big screen."

"That sounds wonderful!" replied Jessica.

She sat down and asked Caleb, "So did anything ever come from our great adventure in the Sand Wash Basin?"

"Well it turns out when they discovered the horses all missing, they investigated and documented a bunch of big rig tire tracks and assumed that someone had stolen the mustangs. I guess the two drunk sheepherders must have figured out a way to escape before the feds arrived to check on the corral."

"That's amazing, what a turn of events!"

"Yeah, I was worried they would find the two sheepherders still there, and there might be a chance they could provide some sort of description of me. Now it appears they would have been the only suspects in what the government agents believe was a simple case of horse rustling."

Jessica chuckled, "That's hilarious."

Angie handed Jessica a glass of wine and sat down beside her exclaiming, "Wow the snow is really coming down now!"

Caleb walked over to the sliding glass doors and looked out at the snow piling up on the deck and commented, "Looks like about six inches already, and the wind is picking up too. I can barely see the trees."

Jessica exclaimed, "Bummer, I just got here and now I'm going to have to leave already."

Angie replied, "Oh heck, why don't you just spend the night. You can sleep on the couch."

"Oooh, that sounds like fun! I'll call home and let him know I'm spending the night."

Michelle piped in, "Will he be mad?"

"Naaa, he's used to me going on road trips for the fashion shows. He'll probably just be happy that I'm not nagging him about getting too drunk with his buddies."

Angie brought in a blanket and said, "Perfect... we'll just drink some wine and watch TV, as long as the power doesn't go out that is."

Michelle couldn't contain herself any longer and blurted out, “Guess what?”

“What?” asked Jessica.

“Parks and wildlife has secretly been preparing some wolves for release, and Caleb and Angie and I are going to get to be there when they do!”

Jessica replied, “Oh cool, I want to go! Do you think they will allow me be there too?”

Michelle thought about it for a few seconds and answered, “We are probably all going to go out in one vehicle, so I don't think they would make a fuss about one extra person.”

“That will be so amazing, I can't wait!”

“I can't either,” added Michelle.

Angie went and got another glass of wine and asked as she was returning to the living room, “Have you checked our web stats lately?”

“No, how are we doing?” asked Jessica.

“Well between the website itself, Instapix, and our Facetime pages, we already have over ten thousand followers and we're barely getting started!”

“Are they upset that we don't have any clothing for sale yet?”

“No, they just seem happy to read our posts. I wonder if we could start a podcast or put on some kind of live fashion show?"

"That would be fun! Would it be just me and you online, or would we try something bigger?"

"Maybe we could start out with just an online show and see how many viewers we get."

Jessica answered, "I'm game, let's get it set up!"

After a few seconds of silence Jessica asked, "So Caleb, how are you doing on your book? What is this one called again, *Thundering Horses* or something like that?"

"*Thundering Hooves*, and I'm in the middle of final review. I should have it published by Christmas."

"Are you going to include our little adventure last month?"

Caleb laughed and said, "No, I don't want to directly implicate us in anything illegal!"

Jessica laughed and replied, "No, I don't suppose that would be a good idea."

The storm steadily intensified, and the whole house shook as the wind howled and snow piled up on the deck. Despite the blizzard raging outside, there was peace and joy inside the house as the four friends snuggled under a blanket and enjoyed their wine and movies.

The Release

Shadow and Ember had eventually become accustomed to their new life in captivity. They didn't understand it, but life was comfortable in their enclosure and the pair was safe from predators and enemy wolf packs. They weren't sure how, but carcasses appeared out of nowhere while they slept. All they had to do was leave the den in the morning and sniff around until their daily meal was located. Ember wondered what had become of her natal family, but she was content with the easy existence provided by their human captors.

Their only fear was the occasional arrival of wildlife specialists, and the sting of a tranquilizer dart. Medical tests were conducted without their knowledge and the groggy wolves would awaken some time later, none the worse for the wear and ready to face another day.

But on this cold snowy December morning, the silence was shattered as a big truck rolled up and a crew of noisy humans spilled out. Soon came the familiar sting of a tranquilizer dart, followed by confusion as the two awoke in the back of the dark truck, separated from each other by the dreaded steel crates. Ember whined and Shadow answered with a quiet woof. The two canines once again squeezed together as closely as they could, for comfort and companionship throughout the ordeal.

Michelle with her three friends, Caleb, Angie, and Jessica, rolled through Steamboat Springs on their way to an unknown location in northwest Colorado. Soon a rough dirt road appeared and they turned northwest, carefully following the lines on Caleb's trail tracker.

"How much further is it?" asked Jessica.

Caleb looked at his display and said, "It's kind of hard to tell, but with this rough road I imagine at least a couple more hours."

"I wonder if the wolves are there already?" asked Michelle.

Caleb replied, "I would think they might not want to drag it out too long after they arrive. I'll bet they get there about a half hour, or maybe an hour before release time."

"I hope we don't miss it," Angie worried.

"We aren't going to miss it. We still have four hours before the release time, and we don't have that far to go, unless we have a breakdown of course."

"The SUV is running well," responded Angie. "All the gauges are holding steady, right where they usually are. We aren't going to break down."

Eventually Caleb announced, "We are really close now, start looking around for the state wildlife crew."

Michelle was looking into the distance with the binoculars and suddenly exclaimed, "I think I see a truck stopped on the side of the road. Wait, there are a bunch of vehicles there."

"That has to be it then," responded Caleb.

"I see the cages!" she squealed exuberantly.

The four friends rolled up onto the scene and were greeted by Heather who ran over and said, "I'm so glad you guys made it! They are making sure the wolves are awake and alert, and are making final preparations to turn them loose!"

“Let's get out!” Michelle exclaimed.

One by one the four friends climbed out of the SUV and approached the wolves.

“Do they have names?” asked Michelle.

“We've been calling them Shadow and Ember. Shadow is the dark one obviously, and Ember gets her name because her eyes are like green fire.”

Caleb knelt down in front of the cages with his camera and snapped a couple pictures for his story.

“How are you boy,” he spoke softly to Shadow. “Please stay out of Wyoming.”

For a moment Shadow stopped fidgeting, and gazed into Caleb's eyes as if he were trying to understand what he was being told. Caleb continued to peer into Shadow's eyes as the two seemed to understand each other as they formed some sort of brief bond.

“I think he likes you,” commented Michelle.

“Yeah I usually hit it off with animals, people not so much.”

Jessica laughed, “Well we like you Caleb.”

Caleb chuckled, “Thank you Jessie, you just made my day.”

Soon the ranger in charge made an announcement with his loud speaker, “Everyone get back behind the cages, we are about to open them up.”

The four friends moved behind the cages and huddled close. The ranger gave the order and both cages were opened at the same time. Shadow burst through the opening, but a confused Ember continued to cower inside. Shadow bolted, but when he realized his mate wasn't with him he returned to her enclosure and coaxed her to come out. Eventually she slowly crept beyond the steel bars, stopping again to look at the crowd behind her. When she saw all the people eagerly urging her on, she turned to the west and trotted away. Shadow turned to follow, but not before locking eyes with Caleb one more time.

"Vaya Con Dios my friend," he spoke softly with a tear gathering in his eye.

Tears of joy were already streaming down Michelle's cheeks, while others appeared to be wiping away tears of their own. Soon the newly freed mates were running west in a full sprint. Not a single member of the crew could look away, or even speak until the two animals were just specks in the distance.

"Well that's it," said Heather. "They are on their own now."

Jessica asked, "Seriously, you don't have any way of tracking them?"

"Oh they have tracking collars, but of the dangers they will face we have no control."

The news crew put down their big camera, while Caleb continued snapping high resolution stills. Eventually he took a seat on the tailgate of one of the crew trucks, when he could no longer see the animals through his big lens. He slumped as if completely drained until Michelle came to join him.

"You okay Caleb?"

"I just never imagined it would be over so quickly. Now it almost seems like it didn't happen, kind of anticlimactic I guess. It seems now my anticipation has been replaced with worry."

"Well, Heather said they had tracking devices so I should be able to keep you informed."

One of the crew suddenly exclaimed, "I have two signals, we are successfully tracking them both!"

Michelle ran over and asked excitedly, "Can I see? Can you show me?"

The technician leaned over to show her the device, and sure enough there were two distinct blips on the screen.

"looks like they have turned north," he mused.

"That's no good," muttered Caleb.

"Oh wait, they are circling back to the east toward the Continental Divide. Hopefully they will find some quiet wilderness deep inside Colorado, where they can be safe while they learn to hunt here and start their own pack."

Eventually the crowd began to disperse and the four friends walked over to reconvene at Angie's SUV.

"Should we get going?" Angie asked as she slid into the passenger seat. "Caleb, can you drive, I'm kind of tired?"

"Sure I can drive," he responded.

As the SUV negotiated the long rough road back to Craig, Angie said "They seemed so small in the distance. I don't know how two lonely wolves can survive in such a hostile expanse."

There was no response from her friends and the journey continued in silence. Eventually Jessica exclaimed, "Hey, I have a signal!"

Caleb continued to grip the wheel, staring ahead in silence at the dirt road while the others all pulled out their phones to check their messages and social media sites. Jessica once again spoke excitedly, "Hey, check this out. A Colorado fashion site is being sued because they only have small sizes, and are being accused of discrimination. Does that mean we would have to carry every size of every item we stock?"

Caleb replied, "Colorado has a long history of being extremely intolerant of small business owner's freedom of expression."

Angie added, "Yeah, the state had been tormenting that baker for years."

"That's why I removed all references to photography services from my website. You can only imagine the kinds of scenarios I might get dinged for refusing to participate in."

"I thought you just didn't like doing it."

"I enjoyed my fashion photography business out in the Bay Area, but those were different times. These days performing artistic services is a mine field, it's just not worth it."

Jessica mused, "Well maybe we want to rethink selling clothes. I don't see how we could afford to stock every size. We might not even be able to get some items in all sizes."

Caleb added, "Even without the discrimination issue, running an accrual business is a pain in the ass. It's mostly big companies with accountants that do that type of business. That's why you see so many brand new clothes in thrift shops as the year ends. Companies have to pay taxes on inventory that they carry into a new year, so they just dump it and deduct the losses. You guys are doing well with your podcasts and try on haul videos., so you might do well to stick to your simple partnership with no employees to worry about, no unemployment insurance, and no medical insurance. Leave those headaches to the big corporations."

Angie replied, "You are probably right Caleb., but I was really looking forward to creating my own clothing designs."

"Maybe you could approach some big corporations and sell your designs to them. Let the big companies handle the retail sales and inventory issues. Kind of like I do with my prints, only on a bigger scale. I don't directly sell anything, as all my sales are made through a third party. They make the sales and collect the taxes, and all I have to do is print the pictures and wait for checks in the mail."

"What do you think Jessie?" asked Angie.

"That sounds like a good idea to me. I'm not looking for a big headache out of this and we are having so much fun doing our podcast, and pictures and videos. Why ruin it with a bunch of accounting problems that we aren't even qualified to deal with?"

"Agreed," responded Angie.

Caleb interjected, "Craig is just ahead, should we look for a place to spend the night?"

Jessica replied, "Craig is boring, let's keep going to Steamboat."

"Yeah," The other two women chimed in.

"Okay, Steamboat it is. Maybe we could get that same hotel where we stayed before."

"Yeah, that was nice!"

Caleb turned off the rough dirt road onto smooth pavement, and accelerated accordingly.

"Oh, that's much better," said Angie.

Michelle added, "Yeah, I was getting car sick trying to look at my phone with all those bumps!"

Eventually the group rolled into Steamboat Springs and Caleb asked, "So, the same place we stayed last time?"

"I really liked the bar there, I think it's worth another stay," replied Angie.

"I'm good with another night there," added Jessica.

Michelle replied, "I guess I'll have to trust all your judgment since I wasn't invited last time."

Caleb laughed, "You are always invited, but we knew you were on the schedule at work. I guess we really didn't ask if you could get the day off, but in our defense you never take a day off!"

"No, I guess I don't do I," she replied.

Caleb parked in front of the hotel and Angie jumped out to run into the lobby. Soon she burst back out of the heavy wooden doors with a big smile on her face, and as she settled into the seat she said, "I got us a room with two double beds."

"That'll work," mused Caleb out loud.

Jessica chimed in, "I have dibs on Caleb!"

"Shut up!" laughed Angie.

Caleb pulled the car into the parking lot and popped the hatch while the three women circled around to grab their bags. Caleb retrieved his as well, and they walked to their room in high spirits.

As they settled in Michelle commented, "I'm going to take a shower before we go out."

The other two women also indicated they would do the same, and Caleb replied "I took a shower this morning, and I haven't really done anything today, so I guess I'll work on my story while you all get ready for dinner."

Eventually the three girls were all dressed and Caleb exclaimed, "Wow, you ladies look hot! But nobody told me were going on a dress up date on this trip!"

"You don't need to dress up, just bring your camera. We aren't going to pass up this opportunity to get some video content for our business," Angie stated emphatically.

"Works for me."

The bar was pretty full by the time the four friends walked in, but fortunately a table was prepared for new arrivals. The hostess met them at the door and pointed to a spot close to the dance floor. "Will this table be okay?" she asked as she pointed toward the dance floor.

"This will be fine," replied Angie as they walked over.

"Can I bring you some drinks?"

"I'll just have a glass of house wine."

Jessica and Michelle both ordered the same, and Caleb asked for a pint of dark beer.

Jessica pointed across the room at a table of young women and commented, "Look, those girls are pointing and staring at us."

"I wonder why," mused Angie.

Pretty soon one of them arose from their table and walked over.

"Aren't you the model podcast women from Denver?"

"We might be," Jessica cautiously answered. "Did you see last weeks episode?"

"You mean the one about how to get an agent?"

"That was us!" replied Angie with a big smile.

The young woman exclaimed excitedly, "Oh my God, I have to go tell my friends!"

Pretty soon the five women scurried over and asked breathlessly, "Will you come and dance with us so we can get some pictures for our Instapix?"

Angie looked at Jessica, who shrugged her shoulders and said "Why not, we can use all the publicity we can get!"

Pretty soon there were seven women on the floor, dancing and shooting selfies with their phones.

Caleb asked Michelle, "Don't you want to get out there with them?"

Michelle laughed, "I think I'll pass."

Caleb pulled out his phone and started shooting video as he commented, "I guess I'd better get some footage, or I'll be in big trouble later."

Michelle laughed, "Such a cross to bear. Well it looks like Angie and Jessie are going to make it with their new business after all!"

"Yes, it seems they are already becoming famous!"

"Good for them!"

After another glass of wine Michelle joined the party, and Caleb's eyes sparkled with pride as he sat back to watch as his entrepreneur wife burn up the dance floor with Jessica, her effervescent sidekick.

"*What a team they are going to make*," he thought to himself as he took another swallow of dark brew.

Christmas Incident

It was a bitter cold morning on the day before Christmas when Michelle walked into the kitchen to start the coffee brewing. She was scheduled to run the north entry at the park later that morning, but there would be plenty of time to open up her laptop and check messages and social media posts. Angie joined her just as the coffee finished brewing, and asked if her if she wanted a cup.

“Sure, is Caleb going to join us?”

“He's already out the door, snowshoeing probably.”

“Have you seen this about Yellowstone?” asked Michelle as she read an article in her news feed.

“No, what are you reading?”

“It's called *Deadliest Season,* it's about the wolf hunt that the Turner administration unleashed on their way out of power,” replied Michelle

“Oh, what does it say?”

“I guess Turner removed wolves from Endangered Species Act protections right before Dolittle was inaugurated, leaving wolf hunts up to the states. By the time Wyoming and Montana got done with their killing seasons, a third of Yellowstone's wolves were dead.”

“Isn't there a law against killing collared animals?” asked Angie.

“Apparently they are fair game. In fact the hunters use the GPS signals from the collars to locate the wolves.”

"That's terrible, does Caleb know about this?"

"I don't know, I imagine he does. I know he keeps up on all that sort of thing," replied Michelle.

"Maybe he just didn't want to upset us, and kept it to himself. We can ask him when he gets back from his run."

"What are you doing today?" asked Michelle.

"I don't know, I guess I'll run up to the mall and see if I can find a couple more little gifts. Want to come with me?"

"I would love to, but I have to run the park entrance today."

"Bummer, I guess I'll give Jessie a call and see what she's doing."

Just then the sliding glass door to the deck opened and Caleb stepped in, carrying his snowshoes.

"Why the long faces?" asked Caleb.

Angie answered, "Did you know about this *Deadliest Season* article about Yellowstone?"

"I know about it but haven't really wanted to think about it, much less talk about it. It's more than I can deal with right now, but on the upside all kinds of lawsuits have been filed by environmental and wildlife groups. Hopefully wolves will soon be put back on the endangered list."

"Are they really just waiting for wolves to leave the park so they can have target practice on them?"

"Yup, just like back when our group used to meet at the Alpine Tap in Bozeman."

"Why would they shoot the very wolves that visitors come from all around the world to see?"

Caleb answered, "I don't know, selfishness, vindictiveness, maybe just plain mental illness. It doesn't even make sense. The environmental tourism industry brings in a billion dollars more than the cattle industry, if you add up all the revenue for the state and surrounding towns. They are shooting themselves in the foot and they are too dumb to understand it, or care."

"Maybe ranchers and hunters can't handle simple math."

"I guess hunters just want to make a name for themselves by killing a Yellowstone wolf. They hate the parks, they hate the wildlife, and they hate the tourists who provide them with the main source of revenue for their state. The politicians know this, but I guess they are too dumb to care as well."

Michelle added, "I wish people would just boycott beef, it isn't even good for people. If nobody bought their products it would take away their leverage with all the crooked politicians."

Caleb replied, "People could at least support a boycott against Wyoming, Montana and Idaho. I would support any boycott that crosses my news feed."

Soon Jessica popped in, cheerfully announcing "The front door was unlocked."

Caleb replied, "Hey Jessie, what are you up to today?"

"Nothing much, I just stopped by to see if Angie wanted to go shopping."

Angie laughed, "I was just getting ready to call you about going up to the mall."

"Cool... I'll drive if you want," replied Jessica.

Michelle commented, "I've got to run off to work, so I'll catch you all later."

"Have a great day Michelle," the three friends responded in unison.

Angie said to Jessica, "We were just talking about the wolf slaughter out in Yellowstone."

"Why are they slaughtering them?"

"I don't know, I suppose some do it for the fur."

"That's terrible, maybe we should try to raise awareness with our fashion site?"

"I guess we could do a faux fur show, to help spread the word."

"That's a great idea Jessie!" exclaimed Caleb.

"That is a great idea," added Angie. "Let's try to get something going, we can start putting out some feelers on our website. Caleb, do you have some animal pictures we can borrow?"

"Sure, just look through my website. Let me know which ones you want, and I'll get them ready for your site. I can also print some big ones that we can hang at your show when the time comes."

"Thank you so much Caleb, that would be awesome!"

"No problem," Caleb said as he stared intently at his phone. "Hey!" he suddenly exclaimed.

"What is it Caleb?" asked Angie.

"My book *Thundering Hooves* just went to active status online."

"What does that mean?"

"I published it earlier this morning and it was just approved. *Thundering Hooves: Spirit of the West* is officially out for distribution!"

Almost in unison, Angie and Jessica congratulated him and Angie rushed over to give him a hug.

"This day has been a long time coming!" exclaimed Angie.

"Congratulations Caleb, I know you worked hard on that book!" added Jessica.

"Wow, it's almost a let down," commented Caleb.

Angie asked, "What do you mean?"

"I don't know, I guess all the work doing the research and writing, the travel and the pictures, the excitement of publishing, and then suddenly it's just done. I've lived that book for over a year, and now it's just done. I have literally given no thought to what comes after the book, and now I'm sort of feeling a sudden void."

Angie replied, "Well don't think ahead just yet. We should go out for champagne breakfast or something."

Jessica leaped to her feet and said, "I'm ready, let's go! That omelet place up by the mall is kind of fancy, maybe they have champagne. I can call up there and see if we need a reservation. What do you think Caleb?"

"Heck yeah, let's go celebrate!" he responded.

"What about Michelle?" asked Angie.

Caleb replied, "You are right, it wouldn't be right to go without her. Tomorrow is Christmas and I know she has the day off."

Angie asked, "Jessie, can you make it tomorrow instead?"

"Sure I can make it tomorrow, but what are we going to do today?"

"How about we crack open a bottle of wine?" offered Caleb.

"Works for me," said Jessica.

Angie laughed, "Why not, after all it is after ten in the morning!"

Caleb said, "I'll go downstairs and get a bottle. I picked up a really smooth plum wine for Christmas, but since we are having champagne tomorrow we might as well drink it today!"

"I love plum wine," exclaimed Jessica.

"That will be fine Caleb, I'll get out the glasses."

Caleb quickly returned with the chilled bottle and opened it. He poured three glasses and handed one to Angie and Jessica, and took one for himself.

"To *Thundering Hooves*," he toasted.

The three clinked their glasses together and took a sip.

"To the wild horses," toasted Angie.

The three clinked glasses and drank once again.

"To a Merry Christmas and a prosperous new year," toasted Jessica.

Three glasses clinked again and the trio sat back to enjoy the moment.

As they basked in the glow of Caleb's achievement, a sharp pop pierced the silence.

"Did you hear that?" asked Jessica.

"I did, it sounded like a rifle shot," replied Caleb.

Two more pops in quick succession prompted Caleb to say, "Sounds like an M16. I'll never forget the sound of that weapon. It's probably somebody's AR."

"It sounds like it's coming from the park. Are people allowed to shoot in Castlewood Canyon?" asked Angie.

"No, there is no hunting allowed in the park. In fact, guns aren't allowed at all there."

"Maybe we should call Michelle," commented Angie.

"I'll try her cell phone."

Caleb picked up his phone and punched in Michelle's number. He let it ring several times but there was no answer. After a few seconds he tried her number again, and this time she answered.

"Hey Michelle, I thought we heard gunfire in the park."

"Yes, it's up here not too far from my booth on the north end. I called Heather and we are shutting down the park. She wants me to go down by the river and investigate."

"Be careful Sweetie."

"I will."

Caleb hung up his phone and said, "There's someone with a gun in the park. Michelle closed the gate and is going down by the creek to check it out."

"That doesn't sound good," exclaimed Angie.

"No, I don't like this at all. I'm going to drive around to the north end and see what's going on."

Caleb laced up his shoes and raced to his truck in the driveway. Several Douglas County Sheriff cars were already making the turn onto Highway 86 when he arrived at he intersection, so he waited for them to pass before making the left turn at Franktown. Soon he was speeding down the dirt road toward Michelle's post, right behind the deputies.

In the meantime, Michelle holstered her weapon and drove over to the north parking lot and trailhead. She checked her radio and proceeded down the trail toward the creek where it sounded like the shots had come from. As she carefully looked around, she heard a woman screaming from the other side of the creek., "Help, somebody help me!"

Just then a man came running up the trail carrying a military style rifle. She drew her service weapon and commanded him, "Put the gun down," but the man kept running toward her.

"Stop, and put down your rifle!"

The man still didn't stop, so Michelle fired a warning shot into the trail near his feet.

At the sharp crack of the pistol discharge, the shooter appeared to regain his senses and stopped running.

"Now throw down your rifle."

"I have the right to carry this gun. I have my second amendment rights."

"Your second amendment rights to carry a gun ended when you drove through my gate. Weapons aren't allowed in a wildlife reserve, so drop it... NOW!"

"The man put down his weapon and she slowly approached to detain him."

"Turn around and put your hands over your head."

She reached for her handcuffs and clamped them around his left wrist. As she reached for his right arm, he suddenly snatched it away and elbowed her in the head. The blow sent her to the ground and he fled without his rifle, running toward the parking lot where his vehicle was parked.

By then two deputies were already running down the trail toward the incident. The perp was violently knocked to the ground as one of officers clotheslined him as the man tried to run past. With one knee on his back, the officer handcuffed the offender and dragged him to his feet to read him his rights."

The other officer was checking on Michelle as a third deputy hustled past to check on a woman screaming on the other side of the creek. As the deputy neared the creek, the woman emerged from the brush sobbing, "He shot my dog!"

"Are you hurt?" asked the officer.

"No it's my dog, he's been shot."

"I'll go check on him, you walk up the hill and join them," as he pointed to the deputy taking Michelle's statement.

Caleb ran towards Michelle, until the officer ordered him to stay back.

Michelle saw him and told the officer that Caleb was her friend, and the officer then motioned for him to proceed.

“Are you okay?” Caleb asked.

The officer replied, “It looks like she is going to have a pretty good shiner for a while.”

Michelle replied, “Yeah, I think my pride is bruised worse than my eye.”

Behind them, a grim faced officer climbed the steep trail from the creek bed, carrying a motionless Siberian husky. As he neared he said sadly, “He was already dead when I located him.”

As the the deceased husky was placed on the ground before the group, the grief stricken hiker collapsed onto his lifeless body with the inconsolable despair that only a dog owner could comprehend.

“Ma'am, do you have someone you would like me to call for you?” asked one of the officers.

She was unable to stop crying long enough to respond, but eventually summoned the strength to barely shake her head, indicating there was no one who could help her.

Paramedics were quickly on the scene to assess the victims, immediately noticing Michelle's rapidly swelling cheek. Another medic approached the dog owner while a nearby officer said, “I think she's in shock. She doesn't seem to be able to speak, but I don't think she's physically injured.”

“Okay, I'll see if I can get her calmed down.”

After examining Michelle's bruised cheek the medic said, "Why don't we get you up to the truck. We can get you some ice packs, and we are going to want to take you in for a quick exam. We have to make sure you don't have a concussion."

"No, I'm okay, I'll be alright."

"Sorry dear, it's protocol. We have to take you in after an incident of this nature."

"I'll follow you," Caleb assured her. "Where are you taking her?"

"We'll be taking her up to the regional hospital in Parker."

"It'll be okay Michelle, I'll be right behind you. Angie and Jessie can drive up and take your car home."

"Okay, I'll see you at the hospital then."

Caleb followed the ambulance and parked outside the ER, where he had seen the ambulance enter. He went in to ask about Michelle, and the receptionist informed him "They are looking at her right now, but I'll let you know when you can go in and see her. Just a take a seat for a little bit while they check her over."

Caleb sat down and pulled out his phone to call Angie.

"Hey Caleb, what's going on?"

"Michelle is gong to have a black eye, but she's okay."

"What, a black eye? How did that happen?"

"There was a shooter in the canyon and he punched her when she tried to cuff him."

"Oh my God, are you sure she's okay?"

"We are up in Parker at the hospital right now, and they are checking her over. Looks to me like she is going to have a black eye but she's able to walk and talk, so I think she's generally okay. She said her pride is bruised worse than her cheek."

"That sounds like her. Was anyone else hurt?"

"The guy shot a woman's dog as they were hiking along the river."

"Oh my God, I hope they throw the book at him."

"Well for sure he's going to be charged with assault on an officer and unlawful possession of a gun in a protected area. It will be up to wildlife officials to charge him with felony animal abuse, but he's claiming he thought it was a coyote."

"That's ridiculous., even if it was a coyote he wasn't supposed to be hunting there."

"Yeah, I imagine that will be taken into consideration, but hunters literally get away with murder around here. A few years ago a guy shot and killed a woman in her driveway. He claimed he thought she was a deer, and got off with a slap on the wrist."

"That makes me so mad, there should be an extra penalty for stupidity. You can bet I'm going to be at his trial to do everything I can to make sure he gets the max."

"I bet you will too! By the way, do you think you and Jessie could drive up to the north entrance and pick up Michelle's car?"

"I don't know, let me see if her spare keys are on the hook."

After a few seconds Angie replied, "Yes we have her spare keys so we'll go pick it up."

"Thanks Angie, I imagine we'll be on our way home shortly."

"Okay, see you then."

Soon a smiling Michelle was wheeled into the lobby saying, "I guess I'm done here. They gave me a prescription for pain and some ice packs, but it's really just a bruise."

"Well that's a relief. Angie and Jessie are going to get your car, but they should be back home by the time we get there."

As Caleb pulled into the driveway, Angie ran out to the car and opened the passenger door to greet Michelle, asking worriedly "Are you okay? Does it hurt a lot?"

Michelle smiled and said, "I'm okay, really it's not that bad."

"Are you sure, do you want me to get you anything?"

"Seriously, I'm okay!"

Michelle snagged the ice packs as she got out of the car, saying "They gave me these ice packs to keep the swelling down."

"Let's get you in onto the couch and we'll fix you up with one."

Jessica greeted Michelle with a big hug at the door and exclaimed, “We were so worried about you!”

Michelle returned the hug and repeated, “I'm okay, it's just a bruise!”

“Well it had to be terrifying, wasn't it?”

“For a little bit I guess, before he put down the gun.”

“What about when he punched you?”

“That happened so fast I didn't really have time to think about it.”

Caleb mused, “I wonder how many people are shot by hunters every year?”

“I don't know, why don't you look it up,” replied Angie.

“Good idea.”

Caleb reached for his phone and typed in the question.

“It says here over a thousand people a year are accidentally shot by hunters, with around a hundred fatalities. The guy who shot a woman in her driveway was charged with manslaughter, but pleaded down to criminally negligent homicide.”

“What's the difference?” asked Jessica.

“I'm looking it up.”

After a few seconds Caleb answered, “Looks like the difference is basically the degree of recklessness. Manslaughter seems to imply simply not caring about your actions, while negligent homicide involves not understanding the possible consequences of one's actions."

Jessica added, "This guy will probably get off with nothing then, since he didn't kill a person."

Michelle replied, "He will at least get the penalties for hunting in a no shooting zone, and maybe lose his hunting license for a few years."

"Oh okay, well I guess that's something. Hey, did Caleb tell you about our Christmas celebration tomorrow?"

"No, what's going on?"

"Caleb got his book published this morning, and we are going to celebrate with a champagne breakfast in the morning at Pierre's up by the mall. Do you think you will be up for it?"

"That sounds like fun, but I imagine my eye is really going to be a mess in the morning. I think I'm going to have to pass, but you guys can still go, right?"

"Hey Caleb, can you run up to the store in Parker and get us a bottle of champagne? We are going to skip tomorrow and celebrate tonight"

"Sure, no problem, take me about a half hour I imagine."

Caleb was soon back from Parker with a nice bottle of champagne, and went into the kitchen to pop it open while Angie retrieved four wine glasses.

As Angie poured the bubbly she asked Jessica, what are you and Rick doing tonight?"

"Oh, nothing, he had to travel out of town for his job."

"That's sad, on Christmas even?"

"Yeah, some BS about a deadline."

"Well why don't you stay tonight and spend Christmas Eve with us. We can drink and open presents, and watch movies later."

"Well, I guess I did pick up a couple things for you guys. I'll go out to my car and get them."

"No hurry, let's just sit and enjoy our champagne and relax for a little bit, it was a rough day."

"Of course."

Angie held up her glass and repeated the morning's toast, "To Thundering Hooves!"

"To Thundering Hooves," they all repeated together as they clinked their glasses.

As they took a sip Jessica added, "Merry Christmas!"

All four downed their drinks again and Angie asked, "Should we open presents now?"

"Sure," responded her friends in unison.

"Let me run out to the car and get mine," exclaimed Jessica.

"Okay, I'll start passing around the ones under the tree," replied Angie.

Jessica put on her shoes and went out into the cold night, while Angie sat beneath the tree reading labels and passing out gifts.

The four close friends each opened their gifts one at a time, until they were all opened and paper was strewn throughout the living room.

"Let me help you clean this up," said Jessica.

"Okay, wasn't that fun?" exclaimed Angie.

"Thank you guys so much for having me over. I really didn't want to spend Christmas alone."

"Of course Jessie, you are like family to us. We wouldn't think of leaving you alone on Christmas!"

Michelle picked up the remote and asked, "Should we watch some more Christmas movies?"

Eventually the little group became drowsy from the champagne and the days excitement and Angie announced, "Well that's about it for me, I'm about to fall asleep!"

Michelle took a couple of aspirin and said, "Yeah, I'm going to bed too."

"Caleb, will you go get Jessie a blanket?"

"I can just sleep on the couch." offered Jessica.

"Of course honey, Caleb will get you a blanket and a pillow."

Caleb returned with a heavy blanket and Angie spread it out on the couch for Jessica.

"Good night all!" exclaimed Caleb.

"Good night and Merry Christmas" replied Jessica.

"Merry Christmas Jessie!"

Hope Eternal

The snow was still quite deep on this beautiful sunny Wyoming early spring morning, and a young wolf stepped carefully on the crusty surface as she tried to avoid falling into the deep drifts. The pup was traversing the snowfield to reach the trees where the snow wasn't so deep, and she would have a better chance of catching a rabbit for breakfast.

She paused and perked up her ears when she heard a strange noise in the distance, and hastened her trek across the snow. As the noise grew louder the alarmed animal began to run. The distance buzz soon became a terrifying roar, and the spirited pup sprinted as hard as she could for the cover of dense pines in the distance. Try as she might, the snow was too deep for her to outrun the powerful snowmobile and she was soon overtaken. Her agility was the next most effective weapon in her capabilities and she tried a sudden change in direction away from the motorized menace. The exhausted wolf charged ahead in the opposite direction as she desperately tried to save herself.

But the two legged monster on the death machine was relentless and tireless. The cowardly hunter soon caught up again and this time there was no escape. Her strength was gone and she was no longer able to avoid the terrifying steel monster. Suddenly the beautiful blue Wyoming sky was replaced by the crunching grinding track of a machine designed to pummel snow into submission, not living flesh. The terrified wolf felt her bones cracking as she was crushed under the 500 pound mechanized predator. She soon lost consciousness as shock from unbearable pain overcame her ability to bear such a brutal experience.

However she was quickly jolted back into consciousness when the man grabbed her by the throat and yanked her broken and defenseless body out of the blood stained snow. All she could do was try to sink her teeth into her ruthless attacker, but suddenly her jaws were sealed shut when the lawless beast violently taped her mouth shut with duct tape. Searing pain quickly sent her back into shock again when she was ruthlessly tied with rope and thrown on the back of the snowmobile.

She drifted in and out of consciousness as her shattered body was overcome with pain each time the speeding vehicle plowed through deep snowdrifts. Suddenly the horrific roar stopped, and a brief moment of relief came to a violent end when the bearded miscreant untied her and once again yanked her to her feet. She tried to run, but piercing waves of pain from broken ribs would barely allow her to breath, much less try to escape.

When she was unable to stand by herself, the man grabbed her by the scruff of the neck and dragged her into a strange building filled with people. A bar full of sadistic drunken patrons cheered and jeered the injured wolf, all the while egging the man on to take selfies and video. The crowd eventually lost interest and the beautiful pup's crushed body lay lifeless on the floor, bleeding out for hours while her tormentor joked and bragged about himself to his callous audience. One last time the dying creature was yanked to her feet and dragged outside where a bullet ended her brief life.

The smell of fresh coffee wafted into Michelle's nostrils as she rolled over to turn off her alarm. She threw on her robe and walked into the kitchen, where she found Caleb staring intently at his laptop.

"Caleb, aren't you going for your morning run?"

"I was just going to check my emails real quick, but my news feed is filled with this story about a Wyoming guy who tortured a wolf pup."

"What, how did he get a wolf pup?"

"It turns out he ran it down with a snowmobile and instead of quickly putting it out of it's misery, he took it into a local bar to show it off. Apparently there were a bunch of people in the bar shooting video and pictures, which eventually showed up on the internet."

"That's awful, what are they going to do about it?"

"Not much so far. He was just fined for unlawful possession of a wild animal and let go."

"That's a slap on the wrist."

Caleb replied, "Yeah, I guess word of the incident has gotten out all over the world and a lot of people aren't satisfied with the punishment. Prosecutors are looking into ways to charge him with felony cruelty, but apparently this kind of thing is not uncommon in Wyoming."

"I hope they nail him to the wall." exclaimed Michelle.

"Good morning," said Angie as she entered the room. She poured herself a cup of coffee and asked, "What's going on?"

Caleb and Michelle filled her in on the details and she commented, "I'm not surprised. There were always a bunch of jackasses coming into the Tap up in Bozeman, bragging about all their killing conquests."

"Constantly," replied Caleb. "I remember when your wildlife group had to come and bail me out of jail for letting a dog out of a trap."

"I remember that too, you made quite a name for yourself among the local hunters up there."

"Yeah, I wasn't too popular in some of the local haunts," chuckled Caleb.

"Well I have to get to work," said Michelle. "Do you guys mind if I pour the rest of the coffee into my travel mug?"

Angie nodded and Caleb motioned for her to take it.

"Okay thanks guys, have a great day!"

"Try to stay out of trouble today!"

Michelle laughed, "That's pretty easy to do most days when I'll be lucky to see ten cars come through the north gate. I doubt we'll see a repeat of any dog murders today."

Angie took another sip of her morning brew and commented, "Maybe this would be a good time to put on our faux fur show. By the time we get it all set up it will be time to show fall and winter fashions."

"Maybe you could donate part of the proceeds to some animal welfare charities. That might bring in a few people that might not normally attend."

Angie replied, "That's a good idea, we might also be able to help out with support for the Denver fur ban."

"What, Denver has a fur ban?"

"Yeah, they succeeded in getting a fur ban for the city of Denver on the ballot this fall. I guess it's based on the ban that Boulder passed a couple years back. If the voters approve, it will be illegal to sell fur in Denver."

"I guess we will find out how far out of the 1800's Denver has managed to progress. I'm not optimistic," commented Caleb.

"Hopefully enough money comes into the campaign to offset all the negative advertising from the hunting lobby. I'll talk to Jessie, and we can start making some calls."

A few days later Angie and Jessica arranged a meeting with the facility manager at the mall, and met in the food court for last minute preparations.

Angie commented, "Oh my God Jessie I'm nervous, how about you?"

"Yeah, this will be our first big show. I hope they take us seriously!"

"We're about to find out, let's go!"

The two entrepreneurs walked the length of the mall to the facilities office and knocked on the door. They waited nervously for a few seconds, and soon the door swung open.

"Hi, you must be Angie and Jessie!"

"That's us," responded Angie.

"I've been following your company online for awhile, so it's nice to finally meet you in person! By the way, I'm Donna and I'm the facilities manager here at the mall."

"It's nice to meet you too!"

"I understand you want to organize a fashion show here in our facility."

"Yes, we want to do a faux fur fashion show to raise funds and awareness about how fur bearing animals are treated. And we want to donate a portion of the proceeds to animal welfare groups."

"That's awesome! I think we can work something out, and maybe the mall can donate some funds for your cause as well."

"That would be amazing!"

The three women worked out the details for a show to be performed in late August, just in time to advertise new fall and winter arrivals.

As they departed the building Angie exclaimed enthusiastically, "I can't believe how well that went!"

"I know, and I can't believe she actually knows who we are!"

"I know, right? Well I guess we're committed now, so we'd better get busy finding some businesses to participate!"

Jessica added, "I wonder if we could include some of our own designs?"

Angie laughed, "I guess we'd better get busy creating some designs if we want to do that!"

"I know, I'm so excited! I'm going to go right home and start working on something."

"Okay, while you do that I'll make some calls and see if I can find some participants."

Caleb was still sitting at his desktop when Angie walked through the front door and he blurted out, "My Facetime feed is flooded with posts about the tortured wolf. The online community has given her the name Hope, and animal welfare groups are offering thousands of dollars of reward money for information leading to a cruelty conviction."

"Wow, sounds like it's really blowing up!"

"Yup, maybe we should donate some money."

"Yeah maybe, but guess what!"

"What?"

"We got a contract for our fashion show at the mall!"

"That's great Angie, congratulations!"

"We are going to donate some of the proceeds to wildlife groups, so maybe we can donate some to Hope."

"That would be amazing, this guy seriously needs to face some jail time."

"Maybe you should write an article about it."

"It looks like it's already getting plenty of press, but I am getting an idea for a new book."

"Cool, what's it going to be about?"

"Well I'm not sure, but it looks like the Republicans are getting set to unleash a veritable war on the wildlife we've been working to save all these years. Maybe I can document all their different tactics to undermine the Endangered Species Act. And maybe I can track the progress of the wolf reintroduction project here in Colorado."

"Sounds like that would be right up your alley."

"Yup, I'll start writing down some notes and see if I can come up with enough material for a book."

"That's a good idea. I'm sure you can do it, you always have."

"When is your fashion show?"

"It's tentatively set for late August. We are supposed to be receiving the full contract in the mail, along with dates and times."

"Great, let me know if there's anything I can do!"

"Oh don't worry, we are going to have plenty for you to do," laughed Angie.

Caleb chuckled and replied, "I thought you might."

Trouble at Elk Creek

Following a winter of exploration on Colorado's western slopes, Shadow and Ember eventually discovered a bountiful valley on the banks of Elk Creek. It was there that they interrupted their travels to make a den where Ember could give birth to her first litter of pups. Before long the time was at hand, and Shadow stood outside the den excitedly awaiting the arrival of his offspring. His only job that day was to protect his mate from danger while she brought their new family into the world. Shadow scanned the woods for predators as he listened for the sound of his newborn cubs. By the time the birthing process was over, Ember had delivered five healthy young wolves into the world.

When all the pups were birthed and breathing she let out a woof to invite Shadow inside, and he carefully crawled through the rocky opening to meet his new family. Wolf pups are the source of great excitement to a pack, and Shadow was as excited as any wolf dad could be. First he licked the face of his mate, and then turned to greet the pups. Ember was already cleaning them up, but Shadow was eager to help. Ember however, had other plans for Shadow. A low growl alerted him that he had other activities to attend to. A new wolf mom expends a lot of energy caring for her new ones and producing milk for them, and for that she was going to require a steady supply of nourishment.

Ember's growl reminded him that for the next few months he was going to be counted upon as the sole provider for his mate, and he immediately set about his task of finding game. An open meadow nearby was his first destination, and he quickly grabbed a rabbit from beneath the tangled mountain grass. Without taking a bite for himself, he returned to the den and laid the catch near Ember's face and quickly departed to catch another one.

Before day's end Shadow had delivered three rabbits and discovered a bison winter kill, still frozen in the creek. He would return for that carcass later in the spring, but for now, rabbits were plentiful and were no match for his speed and power. The new family was safe and well fed, and Ember would not experience danger for some time. She was fortunate to have such a capable mate to care for her, and their location was a secret closely guarded by state wildlife personnel.

Eventually with weeks of successful hunting behind him, Shadow left the den early on a beautiful Colorado western slope morning to catch the day's nourishment. The pups were getting bigger and their appetite was growing voracious. Long days of hunting were required to provide enough food for the growing young ones, who were now eating pieces of meat that Ember shared with them. She instinctively knew that the pups needed to learn that they would be required look for their own food one day, and often hid their food it so they could gain experience with the act of hunting and foraging.

Shadow was an excellent provider but game in close proximity to the den was becoming scarce, and his excursions took him further and further each day. On this day he ventured far from the den, crossing Elk Creek and wandering deep into Grand County. He knew a large kill this far away would require several dangerous treks back and forth to the den, but there was no choice. A pungent odor reached his sensitive scent receptors, coaxing him to change course and investigate. As he neared the source of the strong smell, he also spotted a strange herd of slow moving ungulates, apparently oblivious to his presence. He passed by the stench that had attracted him in the first place, a pit filled with rotting animal flesh of no interest to a capable hunter such as himself.

As he surveyed the situation, the blast of a rifle pierced the dry Colorado air. The deafening noise was accompanied by searing pain in his hindquarters as he spun around and collapsed to the ground. As he tried to stand, his shattered hip gave out and he fell once again to the ground. He could hear men yelling in the distance, an all too familiar sound he now associated with danger and captivity. He knew he had to escape, but it would have to be on three legs.

At first he crawled on his belly nearly incapacitated from the pain, but his will to live eventually overcame the need to rest and tend to his wound. On three legs he ran as fast as he could from the galloping horses, toward the familiar rugged terrain on the other side of the creek. The horsemen reached the creek just as he arrived at edge of the dense pine forest on the other side. Safely in the rocky terrain under the cover of pine trees, he was able to slow his pace and limp back to the den.

Ember greeted him as he whimpered and crawled into the den. She searched for her expected meal, but discovered that the blood she smelled was oozing from Shadow's wound. The once mighty hunter now crawled helplessly into the darkness to lay down beside his excited pups. Ember joined him and licked his wound, the only medicine she knew.

The pack would have no nourishment that night, and by morning Shadow had not moved. Ember understood that she would now have to shoulder the responsibility of hunting for her pups, herself and Shadow too. She gave the command for the pups to stay in the den, and ventured out into the rugged wilderness in search of prey. She soon learned what Shadow already knew, small prey near the den had become scarce. She quickened her pace and expanded her search far beyond familiar territory.

A wolf can travel many miles in a day, and Ember journeyed to the limits of her ability. She knew full well that her family was counting on her. Eventually she caught the scent of deer in the distance, and quietly made her way toward what she hoped would be a successful kill. The mother deer was feeding on mountain grass with her two fawns, born earlier in the spring. The fresh mountain breeze was blowing in Ember's favor, whisking her scent away from the deer and slightly muffling the sound of her stealthy approach.

Soon she was upon the trio and mounted her attack. The little group was caught completely unaware, and Ember quickly killed the smaller of the two fawns while the other two animals fled in terror. Fortunately the young fawn was small enough for Ember to carry by herself, and she began the difficult journey back to the den.

Sunlight was fading rapidly when Ember finally reached the safety of their rocky home. Her pups joyously emerged from the den and attacked the fresh kill with every ounce of strength their tiny bodies could muster. Ember paid them no attention as she began to tear her prey into pieces that the young ones could manage with their small teeth. She also ripped off a big piece of flesh and took it inside the den for her mate. Shadow whimpered his thanks and weakly nibbled his portion.

Weeks passed, and Shadow slowly healed and grew stronger. He eventually emerged from the den, finding his hind leg nearly useless. But he was a strong willed animal that was not going to let the injury incapacitate him forever. Finally came the day when he felt confident enough to leave Ember and the pups behind, and resume the responsibility of providing food. Ember remained at the den and went about the task of teaching the pups to hunt for themselves.

Shadow made his way through the rugged mountain terrain in search of prey and eventually came across a small herd of elk, including several cows and their calves. He crept closer until he felt confident that he could safely snatch one of the smaller calves. He lunged with all the strength his three legs could generate, but the elk calf was faster. The cows instinctively charged toward the bellowing calf, and Shadow was forced to retreat. Undaunted he continued his hunt, eventually coming across a big jack rabbit. He gave chase and nearly exhausted himself in an unsuccessful effort at an easy kill. A mule deer fawn escaped his efforts in the same manner, and he eventually found himself on the banks of Elk Creek.

He remembered well the danger he had encountered here before, and his thoughts were to return to the den with nothing to show for his effort. However his instinct to find prey was stronger, and he remembered the slow moving creatures grazing on the other side of the river. This time he would not approach in the light, hoping that he could kill one of the dull witted animals under the cover of darkness.

The horsemen were nowhere to be seen, but Shadow was not going to take a chance. He hid in the tall grass and waited for the sun to go down. Eventually darkness cloaked his approach and he lunged at one of the calves, killing it almost instantly. He would be unable to drag the entire calf back to his den with only three good legs, so instead tore off a manageable piece and laid it aside.

He buried the remains of the animal as best as he could, using loose dirt and mountain grass to hide his kill for a return to it the next day. Soon he was on his way back to the den with the bounty. In the meantime, Ember had done the best she could to satisfy her young pack by catching small rodents, which she hid for her pups to practice their hunting skills.

Cowboys discovered the kill in the morning while riding the perimeter of the range and one of them yelled to the other, "Jacob, check this out. Looks like something got one of the calves."

"Looks like the work of a wolf."

"Probably one of those damn Elk Creek wolves that the liberals in Denver have saddled us with."

"What should we do?"

"I don't know, I guess we leave it here and bring in the state wildlife people to confirm it."

"Supposedly we are going to get reimbursed if the wolves bother our herd."

"All right then, give them a call and see if they can come out today."

Eventually state wildlife people arrived and confirmed the wolf kill, blaming the Elk Creek Pack for the first wolf depredation in nearly a century. Although Shadow tried his best to catch prey close to the den, his wounds often limited his success. Several times over the next few weeks he was forced to return to the creek, and the easy prey in the meadow on the opposite bank.

The Photoshoot

Angie, Jessica and Michelle were already at the house when Caleb returned from a long day of photography in the canyon. He climbed the stairs to the deck and entered through the sliding glass door, grabbing a bottle of mineral water from the refrigerator before sitting down at the kitchen table.

"Why the long faces?" he asked.

Michelle answered, "They found the first wolf depredation out in Grand County today, and they are blaming the new Elk Creek Pack."

"Based on what?" asked Caleb.

"As far as we can tell, it's just a rancher's word."

"How do they know that the wolf killed the animal, what a cow?"

"Yes it was a cow, and and it appears the state is going to kiss the ranchers ass and pay him for the loss."

"That just pisses me off so much. Those ranchers lose a hundred times as many cattle to disease, exposure to weather, neglect, and any number of things. The state should have never agreed to pay them anything. They are going to use that as a business model from now on."

Michelle replied hopefully, "Well maybe this will be the only one."

Caleb commented, "Did they tell you anything else at your job?"

"No, it seems they are pretty tight lipped about it."

"Aren't you still on the wolf reintroduction team?"

"Yes, but I'm not privy to the politics of it all. I'm just one of the biologists who got to participate in the release."

"Maybe I can find something online."

"I hope so," replied Michelle.

Angie asked Caleb, " I know you are busy Caleb, but can you help us with a photoshoot at the mall tomorrow? We need some pictures for advertisements."

"What time tomorrow?"

"After lunch sometime."

"Maybe we can grab some lunch in the food court before we start."

"I'm in!" exclaimed Jessica.

"Works for me," added Angie.

"I'll just be bored out of my wits, stuck at the park entrance," lamented Michelle.

"When are you going to get promoted out of that crappy duty?" asked Jessica.

"I don't know, I would have thought I'd be on to something more interesting by now."

"I'm sure your time is coming soon," added Angie.

"Well, I gotta run," said Jessica as she arose to depart.

"Okay Jessie, I'll see you tomorrow. What time do you want to meet at the food court?"

"How about if I just meet you here at the house, and we can carpool."

"Sure, be here about noon then?"

"Yep, see you then," she said as she walked to the front door.

By then Caleb had already started up his desktop computer to begin researching the Grand County cattle depredation.

After a few moments of silence Caleb asked Angie, "So what is this photoshoot tomorrow going to entail?"

"We want to shoot some outfits in the mall with all the shops in the background. Do you need any special equipment for that?"

"No problem.. I'll use a couple of off camera strobes, and balance them with the ambient light in the mall. A fast lens should make some nice background bokeh for a nice classy magazine style look."

"That would be awesome Caleb!"

"I'll round up my gear tonight. Am I carpooling with you and Jessie in the morning?"

"I think we can all fit in my car with no problem."

"Okay, .I'll load my stuff in your SUV in the morning then."

Just after lunch Angie pulled into the mall parking lot near the food court. Heads turned when Angie and Jessica walked in, already dressed in their first look.

Even though his friends were oblivious to the stares, Caleb noticed all the attention and commented, "This should be a great show, you already have the full attention of your fans!"

Angie finally looked around and quickly noticed all the eyes upon them.

"Well okay then, I guess we'd better do good!" commented Angie.

Angie picked up her phone and gave Donna a call.

"Hi Donna, we're already here in the food court. Where do you want to meet?"

"I'll just come down there and sit down with you for a few minutes. After you eat we can all walk over to the shooting area together."

"Sounds good, do you have some kind of cart for Caleb to wheel his lighting gear in?"

"I'll have maintenance bring one over."

Soon it was time for the shoot, and a small but curious crowd was already gathering. Caleb took a couple of test shots, and waved to Donna that he was ready.

Angie walked out first, wearing designer blue jeans and a white faux fur jacket. She noticed some disapproving glances and stopped to make an announcement, “Greetings folks, we are getting some pictures to advertise our faux fur fashion show next month right here in the mall! Proceeds will go to wildlife groups working hard to ban animal fur here in the Denver area. And don't forget to vote for the ban in November!”

Many in the rapidly growing crowd clapped, and Angie felt comfortable continuing the photoshoot. Jessica was next on deck, wearing a long skirt and imitation leather jacket. The crowd was now supporting the event, clapping enthusiastically each time the women walked in with a new outfit. Eventually Donna announced that the models were taking a break, and asked Caleb if she could see the pictures.

Caleb responded, “Sure,” and turned his camera around. Donna looked delighted as she thumbed through a couple dozen images. In the meantime Angie and Jessica crowded in close, also doing their best to see the pictures on the back of Caleb's camera.

Finally Donna declared triumphantly, “I think we got it! Caleb... when can you get these delivered?”

“I'm sure I can have them done by the end of tomorrow. Do you want me to drop by on a thumb drive?”

“Sure, I'll be here until six. Why don't you stop by my office around five.”

“I'll be there!” he said confidently.

After a few moments of silence Angie said to Caleb,“We are going to change, so why don't you start packing up.”

"Okay, can you drive your car up to the door when you are ready? I don't want to lug this stuff all the way across the parking lot again."

"You got it."

Soon the elated trio was on their way back to Franktown, excitedly discussing the photoshoot.

"Did you see all those people, they were even clapping for us," commented Angie

"That was awesome," replied Jessica. "I think it is going to be a great show, I can't wait!"

"Me too, I think we are going to be able to make a big donation for the wildlife!"

Caleb was quiet in the backseat as he looked through the collection of images again.

"You girls were beautiful today, these pictures are great! The models in the big fashion magazines have nothing over you!"

Both women chimed in at once, "Thanks Caleb!"

As they neared Franktown Caleb suggested that they stop to toast the successful day, "Hey, we should stop at the Stage Line and have a couple of beers!"

Angie replied, "That sounds great Caleb, what do you think Jessie?"

"Works for me!" she replied.

Angie pulled in to the parking lot and the trio walked toward the open door.

"Maybe we should call Michelle," commented Jessica.

Caleb replied, "She's still at work. If we're still here later we can give her a call."

The jukebox was playing country music when they walked into the dark saloon. Most of the tables were available, so they just walked in and sat down. The waitress and a big dude approached their table, but separated as they drew near to the end of the bar. The big guy took a seat at the front door and the waitress came over to take their order.

"Hi guys, how are we all today?"

"We're great," answered an enthusiastic Jessica.

"Glad to hear it! I'm Bonnie, can I start you out with some drinks?"

"Should we just get a pitcher?" asked Caleb.

"Sure," replied Jessica.

"We'll have a pitcher of beer then, whatever you have on tap," said Angie.

"How about our microbrew special of the day? It's a pale ale that a lot of people really seem to like."

"That sounds excellent," replied Caleb.

Angie and Jessica nodded their heads in approval, and Bonnie turned to walk their order to the bar.

Eventually the lively country rock music was interrupted by a slow ballad, prompting Jessica to excuse herself for a restroom break. Angie followed close behind while Caleb continued to sip his brew, and reflect on the photoshoot. He glanced up as the two women returned from the restroom, and noticed a scruffy dirty looking cowboy approaching them from the bar. As the man neared Jessica, Caleb heard him slur a rude invitation, "Hey baby, wanna dance?"

Jessica answered politely, "No thanks."

"What, do you think you are too good to dance with us cowboys?"

"No, that's not it. I'm married and I just don't dance with strangers."

Caleb stood and walked toward the women, while the man angrily turned and walked away. At first it appeared that Jessica had quietly diffused the situation, but suddenly the belligerent slob turned around and stepped back in front of her. Caleb heard him mumble something unintelligible, and quickly approached to intervene. Before Caleb could get positioned, the trouble maker tried intimidating her by lifting his fist to her face. Caleb didn't wait to see what would happen next, and responded with a powerful right jab to the chest which sent the attacker reeling twelve feet across the bar. Angie heard the sound of cracking ribs and exclaimed, "Oh crap Caleb, I think you broke his ribs."

The cowboy eventually landed on his back and made no move to get up. The bouncer responded quickly to the altercation and said to Caleb,

"I saw the whole thing and I would have done the same thing, so you're good. That guy is always causing trouble in here so I'm going to 86 him as soon as he comes around. Go ahead and enjoy yourselves, and sorry for the trouble."

Caleb thanked him and he and the women sat back down to finish their beer.

"Well damn," said Jessica. "That was exciting!"

Angie chuckled, "I don't know if exciting is what I would call it."

They eventually finished the pitcher and decided to pay their tab and call it a day.

"I guess we aren't going to need to call Michelle after all," commented Jessica.

"No I guess not. She should still be at work, or at least she's supposed to be. Earlier she didn't sound too excited about sitting in the booth all day."

"She didn't, did she," replied Angie.

"I wonder if she is going to look for something else soon?" wondered Jessica.

"I wonder if she would want to join our little company and work with us," commented Angie.

"Maybe so," replied Caleb.

The three friends quickly forgot about the unfortunate incident in the bar and climbed into Angie's SUV. They drove the rest of the way in silence, each lost in their own thoughts.

Evidence on Elk Creek

On a sweltering August evening in central Colorado, Angie and Caleb were enjoying a movie in their air conditioned living room when Michelle came home from work.

"Hey Michelle, how was your day?" asked Caleb.

"Boring," she replied. "What are we watching?"

"Caleb insisted on watching this sniper movie before it goes away."

"Cool," replied Michelle as she sat down on the couch on the other side of Caleb.

During a break in action in the movie, Caleb mentioned that he was thinking of going out west to investigate the recent cattle depredations.

"Think I might go out to Steamboat and see if I can find out anything about the Elk Creek wolf pack cattle depredations. I heard the rancher had a carcass pit that was drawing in predators."

An enthusiastic Michelle chimed in, "Oh, I want to go!"

"Oh, I don't know honey, it could get a little dicey if I get spotted by the lookouts."

"Oh please Caleb, I won't get in the way!"

"Well, maybe there is something you can help me with. I need someone to drop me off near the trailhead so I can hike in and take a look at the ranch on the other side of Elk Creek."

"I can do that, please let me come along!"

"Okay, but then I need you to just go back to Steamboat and wait until I call. I don't want anyone to see my truck anywhere near the trailhead."

"I don't mind, I can keep myself busy in Steamboat until you call."

"Okay, can you get a few days off next week?"

"I have a lot of vacation time saved up, I don't think it will be a problem to get as much as I need."

"Okay, how soon can you get it approved?"

"I'll call Heather right now."

Michelle dialed her phone and Heather quickly answered, "Hi Michelle, what's up?"

"Hi Heather! Hey, I was wondering if I could get some time off next week. Caleb needs my help with something."

"I think that would be fine. I have a new guy who has a new baby on the way and needs to bank some extra money. He's been begging for extra hours, so I think he'll be glad to fill in."

"Okay, can he cover me for a few days starting on Monday? I'm not exactly sure how much time off I'm going to need."

"I'll check with him real quick, can I call you right back?"

"Sure, I'm not going anywhere today."

It was less than a minute before Michelle's phone rang again,"Hi Heather, what did he say?"

"He was happy to take your shift for the week, so go ahead and enjoy yourself! What trouble is Caleb trying to get into now?"

"Oh no trouble, he just needs me for some of his photography stuff."

"Okay, have fun then!"

"Sounds like you have the week off then?" Caleb asked.

"Yes, Heather said it was no problem for me to take the entire week."

"Alright then, let's plan to leave on Monday. I'll call and get us a hotel room in Steamboat."

"Oh, thank you Caleb, I'm so excited!"

Angie laughed and said, "Somebody must be really bored at work!"

"Oh my God, you have no idea," replied Michelle.

"Are you off tomorrow as well?"

"Yes, I have the whole weekend."

"Okay then, we'll go up to RSI and get some supplies. I need to be prepared for several days of solo wilderness camping."

"Maybe I can pick up some snacks for hanging out in the hotel room."

"Of course, we'll make sure you have everything you need," affirmed Caleb.

Monday finally arrived with Caleb and Michelle on the road early, cruising into Steamboat Springs by lunchtime.

"What do you say we get some lunch before we get checked into the hotel?"

"Sounds good, it doesn't have to get anything fancy. Fast food is fine with me."

"No worries, it's no problem to get a decent meal somewhere. What do feel like today?"

"How about pizza? I've been craving a good pizza for a while now."

"Pizza it is then," replied Caleb as he consulted his phone for a nearby pizza place.

"There's an Italian style tavern just down the road. It wouldn't be right to have pizza without a good beer to wash it down."

"Excellent!" replied Michelle.

They walked into the tavern together and were seated by the

hostess. Soon they were sipping dark German beer from the tap while they waited for their meal to be served.

"So Caleb, what's your plan once you get to Elk Creek?"

"I'm going to have you drop me off a few miles downstream, and I'm going to hike in from there. You will drive straight back to Steamboat before anyone sees you, and wait for me to call."

"What if your phone dies?"

"I have a big auxiliary battery for my phone that's supposed to last for several days. Just to be safe, I'll turn it off to save power until I need to check messages and make calls."

"Okay, but just in case shouldn't we set a hard turnaround time for me to meet you at the trailhead?"

"That's a good idea, if I don't call by Thursday morning, come to the drop off point to see if I'm there. But I don't think it's going to be a problem, I also have my satellite phone if my cell doesn't work. I should be able to communicate with you regularly throughout the week"

"What's your plan once you find the ranch?"

"My plan is to find out if there's really a carcass pit, and see if there are any ranch hands staking it out for wolves. If there is a pit, I want to get pictures of it for the media. They are supposed to be using non-lethal methods to scare away predators, so if they aren't maybe we can throw a wrench into their reimbursement claims."

"Aren't you worried they are going to catch you?"

Caleb laughed, “I think if I can outwit a whole platoon of Taliban, I should be able to stay ahead of a couple of cigar puffing ranchers.”

“Well it has been a while since the war you know.”

“I know, but I've kept up with my skills and physical conditioning.”

“I know, but I'm still worried.”

“It'll be okay, I promise.”

They finished their meals in silence and waited for the server to return with the check..They paid the bill and as they were walking out, Michelle suggested “Let's get checked into the hotel. Are we staying at the usual place?”

“That was the first place I called!”

“I hope you got the single again. You aren't going to be here most of the time, and it will be cheaper.”

Caleb, now deep in thought about the task ahead of him eventually replied, “Yes, I got the same room as we had last time.”

Michelle waited in the truck while Caleb took his credit card to the front desk. Soon he returned with the receipt and said,“We're all checked in, I'll pull up closer so we can unload.”

After moving their bags to the room Michelle lamented, “We should have picked up some beer.”

“Yeah, we'd better run out and get some. It might be a long week for you without some bottled comfort. I can run out if you want to wait here."

"Okay, while you do that I'm going to unpack a few of my things and take a shower."

Caleb soon returned with a case of brew and cracked one open for Michelle and himself. She fiddled with her phone charger while Caleb tested the batteries in his sat phone. She turned on the television and leaned back on a pillow on the love seat to watch a show she liked. Caleb eventually joined her, leaning his head back as Michelle snuggled close. Both were soon sound asleep as the TV droned on through the night.

Morning found them in the same position when Caleb's eyes fluttered open to greet the sunrise. He took a sudden deep breath, as the gravity of the task ahead sank into his mind. Michelle clutched his hand and said, "Do we really have to do this? Can't we just hang around in Steamboat and relax for a few days?"

"Hopefully I'll get this all done today, and we can have some fun for the rest of the week while I write the story."

"Well let's get it done then, cowboy!"

Caleb chuckled, "I'll certainly try! What do you say we hit the complimentary breakfast bar real quick, and get this show on the road. I imagine it's going to take two or three hours to get to the trailhead."

Soon they were on their way with Michelle at the wheel. Caleb plugged his phone into the charger and fiddled with GPS coordinates, eventually sending them to Michelle's phone once he had them dialed in.

"I sent you the coordinates for Elk Creek, where I expect to encounter the carcass pit."

"Okay, hopefully I won't need them."

"I don't expect that you will, but you have them just in case."

After they had been on the road a couple hours Caleb commented, "I think we're almost there. According to my app there should be a small parking lot on the left side of the highway."

While Caleb was looking down at his app Michelle exclaimed, "There's a trailhead, is that the one?"

"It sure is, do you need to add a pin to your maps so you can get back here?"

"Naaa this was easy to find. I won't have any trouble finding it again."

"Okay, pull in and I'll get my stuff out of the camper topper."

Caleb was soon geared up and ready to begin the long trek to Elk Creek.

"Okay I guess I'm ready, hopefully I'll be able to stay in touch."

Her face clouded with dread as she she reached out to give him a hug.

"You be careful Caleb, don't do anything stupid."

He laughed and replied, "When have I done anything stupid?"

Michelle stuck her finger in his chest and said, "Don't get me started or we'll be here all day."

His face suddenly became serious as well and he replied, "I suppose so, but please don't worry. I'm going to slip in, get the pictures, and slip back out without anyone knowing I was even here."

"Okay good luck, I'll be waiting for your text messages!"

She watched with great trepidation as he disappeared into the pine forest. When he was out of sight, she climbed back into the truck for the drive back to Steamboat.

Caleb stopped and took a deep breath as he climbed the steep ridge before the long descent into the Elk Creek valley. His enthusiastic charge up the hill left him oxygen depleted, and he soon needed a short rest to help him recover and organize his thoughts. Now that he was on the trail, it was a little easier to calculate what he would be up against for the rest of the hike. It would be a two mile climb up the ridge, followed by a series of rocky switch backs to the river bed. At a steady pace of three miles per hour, he estimated an arrival at the creek bed by early afternoon.

As he strode up the mountainside, he took a long drink from his water bottle and unwrapped an energy bar for a few bites. Step by step he made his way to the summit, where the a vast valley opened up before him. He thought to himself, "*I can see why the wolves would settle here, it's magnificent!*" The climb down the backside of the ridge was less strenuous, but he continued cautiously as the rocky trail was difficult to negotiate and he didn't want to twist an ankle. A few more treacherous foot steps down the trail dispelled any illusions he might have had about making it back to Steamboat today.

Once his mind was free of the self imposed time constraint, he settled into a steady gait that would put him on schedule to reach the valley by late afternoon. He continued to pick his way through the rocks, stopping occasionally for a drink and a bite of energy bar. Eventually the trail flattened out, and based on the time of day Caleb assumed he was nearing his destination. He hoped he wouldn't have to search too long for the ranch and carcass pit, but decided not to dwell on things that were out of his control.

The sound of gurgling water soon reached his ears, and he surmised he was near the banks of Elk Creek. The dense pine forest gave way to lush green grass and a valley with an unimpeded view of the opposite bank. A comfortable looking rock behind good cover beckoned to him, "*A good place to get out the binoculars to survey the situation,*" he thought to himself.

As he watched, two men approached on horseback and took up positions where they could watch the dense forest on his side of the creek. As Caleb scanned the scene before him, it became apparent that the two ranch hands were posted at some kind of man made depression in the dirt. "*Is that the carcass pit?*" he quietly wondered.

Caleb remained quiet and motionless as he watched and waited. Eventually darkness descended upon the valley, and the men mounted up and rode away. After pumping some water from the creek with his filter, he retreated back into the trees to look for a couple of aspen that he could use to hang his tarp. He soon found a relatively flat spot between two trees and set up camp. The first order of business was to fire up his little one burner propane stove to heat some water for a bag of freeze dried stew. As he enjoyed his food, the mournful howl of a wolf reached his ears. "*Is that Shadow and Ember singing to each other?*" he wondered.

He checked his cell phone to see if there was a signal by chance, but there was nothing. No browsing the internet to pass the time on this long dark evening. He thought of Michelle back at the hotel, and of Angie at home and imagined,"*I'll bet Jessie is over tonight and they are working hard on the fashion show.*" He chuckled to himself as he pictured them off to a good start, soon distracted by a cold bottle of chardonnay. "*At least I can send out a text message with my sat phone*," he thought.

He reached into his pack and pulled out his bright LCD headlamp, followed by the sat phone. First he sent a message to Michelle, "I made it down to Elk Creek late this afternoon, and two men on horseback showed up as I was watching. They seemed preoccupied with an unusual looking depression in the ground which is probably the carcass pit. They were also watching the forest on my side of the creek, probably waiting for Shadow."

He then sent another message to Angie, "All good so far. I'm camped in the river valley, and hope to get pictures of the pit in the morning. Thought I might have heard Shadow and Ember singing a few minutes ago."

Angie wrote back first, "Good to hear from you Caleb. Glad you are safe tonight, please be careful!"

Michelle was next, "Good Caleb, so do you want me to head back up early in the morning?"

"No, wait for me to message. I don't really know how long this will take me tomorrow."

"Okay, I'll wait to hear from you then. Stay safe!"

"I will."

Caleb reached into his pack and pulled out a pint of of smooth whiskey to help him drift off to sleep. He turned off his headlamp and leaned back on his pack to gaze at the Milky Way. The stars were so dense in the darkness they appeared as a solid white canopy. "*It doesn't get any better than this,*" he thought to himself. He eventually drifted off to sleep to the soothing sound of wolf song, and a slight breeze blowing through the tall pines above.

His eyes popped open as the sound of chattering squirrels and bird song reached his ears. He drew a sharp breath of cool crisp mountain air, and savored the scent of fresh pine as he unzipped his sleeping bag. Water for coffee and oatmeal was soon warming on the burner as he threw on an extra layer of wool, until the morning sun could warm his shoulders. He wanted to get an early start on pictures before any cowboys could return to the site, so he didn't linger for a second cup of coffee.

He packed up camp and carried his rucksack with him to the riverbank. It was a bit too deep for comfort right there, so he got out his glass to take a look up and downstream. He noticed a bridge of rocks not too far downstream and surmised that they were placed there as part of the trail system. Once on the other side of the creek, Caleb quickly made his way to the pit and was shocked by what he saw. Dead cattle in various stages of decay had been thrown by the dozens into the pit. Some were skeletons while others were just a rotting pile of stinking flesh. The stench was horrific, and Caleb pulled his shirt up over his face to shield his nose from the odor.

Just as he was finishing up with the photography, he heard voices approaching from the north. Assuming they were horsemen coming to check on the pit, he quickly hid himself thinking "*Damn, trapped on the wrong side of the stream. I wonder how long they are going to stay*?"

"Do you see any tracks this morning?" one of the men asked.

"No, I guess they didn't come last night."

"Hey, did you walk around here at all yesterday?"

"Why?"

"I see the boot tracks"

"Probably some hikers, they are crawling all over this place since they put that trail in."

"Yeah, just keep an eye out, they might still be here somewhere."

After a couple long hours of waiting had sorely tested Caleb's patience, the men decided to ride upstream to look for wolf tracks. Caleb took advantage of the opportunity to make his way to the other side of the creek, where he hoped to get back on the trail. But just as he was about to race to freedom under the cover of dense pine on the hillside, the men returned to continue watching for wolves. He spotted a nearby boulder and slipped behind it for cover. "*Oh my God, I hope I'm not stuck here the rest of the day,*" he worried.

From where he was hidden he could clearly hear their conversation,"That wolf hasn't been here for a few days, he's got to be getting hungry soon."

"He'll be back, but. I hope we find him before the state folks do. They are going to find that bullet wound and blame it on us."

"They aren't going to find anything but a collar, a damn long way from here," commented the other ranch hand.

Eventually the men dismounted and tied their horses some distance from Caleb, giving him a chance to sneak across a relatively placid section of river behind some massive boulders. The pine forest was much closer to the creek there, and Caleb quickly scrambled to safety. A steep cliff wall in that area blocked him from climbing out of the valley, and he was forced to slip quietly through the trees past the men, hoping to reach the trailhead undetected.

Just as he turned onto the trail back up the mountain, he heard one of the men yell, "Hey, there's somebody over there!"

Caleb took cover under a downed tree trunk and waited to see what was going to happen.

He could see through the branches that the men had pulled out their rifles, and were searching for him through their scopes. He watched as their line of sight passed over him a couple of times, and once again lamented that he might be stuck there until dark. Just then a beautiful wolf appeared on the trail, hidden from his stalkers by the dense pine forest. Caleb locked eyes with him and whispered, "No, go back."

As he looked closer, Caleb recognized the wolf as Shadow from when they had released him the autumn before. Shadow looked at him curiously and took a step in Caleb's direction. Caleb again whispered, "No Shadow no, go back!" Shadow stopped again and sat down to assess this unexpected encounter. "Shadow, go away, go back!" urged Caleb.

Just then, one of the men yelled, "Hey, I think I see him under that log, do you see him?"

Shadows ears perked up, and Caleb watched in relief as the magnificent animal quickly turned and limped away on three legs. "*Thank God*," thought Caleb to himself as his attention returned to his own safety.

"Let's ride over and check it out," one of the men shouted.

Caleb knew he could not wait around for them to capture him and confiscate his pictures, so he decided at that moment to make a run for it.

"Stop!" he heard the men yell as bullets whizzed over his head into the trees.

But with the safety of the forest only a few yards away, he decided to ignore their commands. He reached the treeline safely, and once concealed by pine branches he chucked to himself, "*Game on boys,*" and the hunted had now become the hunter.

By the time the men had guided their horses through the stream and across the clearing, Caleb was well up the trail and out of sight. He knew the men would expect him to keep climbing so he waited for a rocky section of trail that wouldn't reveal his footprints, and turned off the trail in search of a hiding place. Soon the men galloped past, and Caleb returned to the trail to follow them. Their pace slowed to a crawl when they reached the rocky switchbacks, and the sun began to descend behind the mountains to the west.

Caleb crouched down behind some bushes and spied on them as they slowed to a stop. He heard one of the men say, "He's got to be up there."

"Yeah, but these horses aren't safe on this trail in the dark."

"Maybe we should make camp., whoever that is won't climb this trail in the dark either. We'll start the search again at first light."

Caleb watched as they tied their horses, and set up a makeshift camp in a flat clearing several yards off the trail. Soon he heard one say to the other, "Give me a swig of that."

First the men spoke in anger about the wolves, about how they had shot one and hoped to finish him off before their crime was discovered. As minutes turned to hours, their words slurred and eventually gave way to snoring. Caleb considered sneaking past them on the trail to make his way to the highway in the dark, but even he wasn't eager to negotiate the dangerous climb at night. But he also wasn't fond of the idea of horses pursuing him again either, so he came up with a plan. He figured the men were passed out cold for the night, and wouldn't hear him release the horses. He arose from his hiding place and quietly crept into their camp and cut the animals tethers with his knife. One nickered quietly, but both followed willingly as Caleb led them down the trail.

Once they reached safer terrain below, Caleb turned them loose with a slap on the hind quarters. The horses trotted down into the valley where they could graze on succulent grass on the banks of the creek. Caleb reached into his pack and pulled out his GPS trail finder to look for another trail. A longer but safer route along the river lit up, and Caleb turned upstream along the banks of the river.

After a couple hours he began looking for a suitable campsite, and eventually found one between two suitable aspen trees. Once again, he set up his tarp and boiled water for a hot meal. He laughed out loud when he thought of the fat ranch hands waking up with a hangover, and their horses nowhere to be found. "Good luck getting your fat asses back to the ranch," he chuckled out loud.

He rummaged through his pack and found the bottle of whiskey and his sat phone. He took a couple of swigs as he crafted a message to Michelle, "Hey Michelle, had to camp out again."

Soon came the reply, "Good to hear from you Caleb, are you okay?"

"Yeah, I had a little incident down by the river with the ranchers, but I can tell you for sure I'm better off right now than they are!"

"Oh my God Caleb, what happened?"

“I'll tell you all about it tomorrow..”

“So you want me to head up in the morning?” she asked.

“Yes, only I'm on a different trail now so you are going to have to drive a little further up the road. Look for Elk Creek crossing under the highway, and I'll meet you there.”

“What time?”

'Just start out when the sun comes up, and we'll probably get there at about the same time.”

“Okay, I can't wait to see you! Did you get the pictures?”

“I sure did, but I'll tell you all about it tomorrow.”

“Okay, see you in the morning then.”

The Fashion Show

It was late afternoon by the time Caleb and Michelle pulled into the driveway in Franktown. Jessica's car was there, so they knew the women were either hard at work or taking a break with a glass of wine. Upon entry they discovered it was the latter.

"I see you ladies are hard at work as usual," Caleb joked.

"We're just taking a little break," protested Jessica.

Caleb asked, "How is the show coming along, are you about ready to go?"

Angie replied, "I guess you already know, but we are ready to go for the weekend. We just need to round up a couple more models... speaking of which, are you going to help us out Michelle?"

"Oh golly guys, you know I don't like modeling."

"I know," replied Angie, "But you are a natural, and we need you."

"Oh okay, what do I have to do?"

"Nothing much, just ride up with me and walk the catwalk with whatever we give you to wear. And how about you Caleb, can you shoot for us? I'm sure the mall will have someone filming, but I don't want to have to hassle with usage rights."

"Sure, I can help."

"How was your trip by the way?"

"It went well, I got the pictures anyway."

"So you just walked in and shot the pictures and nobody cared?"

Caleb laughed, "Not exactly, the ranchers eventually spotted me and ran me off."

"And they just let you leave with the pictures?"

"Well they did take a few shots at me as I was escaping, but fortunately they can't shoot for shit. Either that or they were just firing into the hillside to scare me. Sometime in the last couple of months they did manage to hit Shadow though. He's limping on three legs, which probably explains why he's having to resort to killing livestock to feed the pack."

"Bastards," exclaimed Jessica.

"I had the last laugh though, I circled back while they were sleeping and cut their horses loose. They had a really long walk home this morning," laughed Caleb.

Angie laughed, "That sounds like something from your playbook."

Jessica asked, "What are you going to do with the pictures?"

"I'm going to write up an article for the newspaper, and probably send a copy to work with Michelle. The question is whether anyone in charge is going to care. Parks seems intent on kissing the rancher's asses, so I doubt they will force this miscreant to clean up his stinking pit of death."

Caleb spent Friday writing his story while the women wrapped up final details for the show on Saturday, which was rapidly approaching.

Finally on Friday night, preparations for the show were complete. Michelle was home from work, and the three women were already in the living room sipping a glass of wine when Caleb returned from a meeting with the newspaper editor.

"Looks like they are going to publish it on Sunday," he said.

"That's awesome Caleb!" exclaimed Michelle.

"Congratulations Caleb," added Jessica.

"The question is whether anyone is going to read it, way down in the editorial section."

Angie replied, "You know what you always say, "you only need one person to read it, the right person.""

"True enough!" he replied.

"Are you all ready for tomorrow?" Angie asked.

"Yup, I packed up my gear this morning and it's all ready to load up. Are we all riding together, or should I drive myself?"

"I don't think we are going to have room for all of our stuff and your gear too."

"Okay, I'll load up my truck and come separate."

"I'm going to ride up with Caleb then," added Michelle.

"That's fine honey, we will see you there then."

Jessica asked, "Can I just sleep on your couch tonight? My husband is out of town on business and I would rather not have to mess with getting up early to make it all the way down here on time."

"That's fine Jessie," replied Angie. "I'll be glad to have your help first thing anyway."

Caleb was the first to awaken the following morning, and he started the coffee brewing. A bleary eyed Angie soon entered the kitchen, while at the same time Jessica was yawning and stretching on the couch.

Michelle walked into the room and said, "Well, this is it, go time!"

Angie replied nervously, "That it is."

Each of them grabbed a cup of coffee, and Caleb made a few slices of toast.

"I don't guess we have time for a big breakfast but maybe a little toast will soak up stomach nervousness," he commented.

"A piece of toast will be fine for me Caleb," commented Jessica.

"Me too," chimed in Michelle.

Donna was already waiting at the front door with the key when the little caravan arrived.

"Why don't you all put your stuff right inside, and then we'll lock the doors until opening time."

"Cool, Caleb do you want to pull up onto the sidewalk so you don't have to carry your gear so far?" asked Angie.

"Sure, it won't take me long. I don't have that much to carry."

Soon all four partners were inside with their clothing and gear, and Donna locked the big glass doors behind them."

She showed them the runway with curtains at the front and seating on both sides and said, "Well here it is, this is where we're going to run the show. The restrooms are right over there for the models to change, and we will have a couple of assistants on site to help the models with makeup and clothing."

"Sounds perfect," replied Angie.

Caleb commented, "It looks like your hot lights should provide me with plenty of lighting for video. I'll set up a couple of strobes along the runway if that's okay, to put some fill light on the model's faces for the still shots."

"That's fine Caleb," commented Donna. "Why don't we head over to the food court and grab some lunch before we get too busy."

A small crowd was already gathering near the runway when the group returned from lunch. Half a dozen models were milling around the restrooms, while assistants helped them with final touch-up. Caleb took advantage of the pre-show chaos for a few test shots to balance his strobes with the light from the hot lamps lining the runway.

Soon Donna took over the microphone, and Caleb's three friends joined the other models behind the curtains at the head of the runway.

"*Here we go*," he thought to himself.

Angie was the first to emerge from behind the curtains, wearing a long dress with a plunging neckline accompanied by a beautiful faux fur jacket. Donna explained on the microphone that the outerwear used in the show was all faux fur, and no animals had been harmed in their creation. Camera flashes from the audience bathed the runway in bright light as Angie confidently strode down the catwalk. Jessica was next, wearing a sexy cocktail dress accentuated by a beautiful white faux fur wrap draped over her shoulders.

Caleb felt someone touch him on the shoulder, and he turned to discover Michelle standing beside him.

"What are you doing here?" he asked.

"They had plenty of models, so I decided to come and help you. Is there anything I can do?"

"Sure, you can run the video while I shoot the stills."

He quickly showed her the button to start and stop the recording and said, "Don't worry too much about pausing the video, I can cut the clips in post. Just follow the models on their way down the runway, and maybe sweep through the audience if there's a break in the action. Zoom in a bit when the model leaves the curtains, and slowly back off as they get closer to the camera. Got it?"

"Got it!"

"Okay then, you know where I'll be if you have any questions!"

"One by one the models strolled down the runway, and then circled back to the curtains to change into a new look. Eventually all the outfits had been shown, and the crowd clapped enthusiastically. Donna brought Angie and Jessica up front to give them credit for the show, and all the hard work required to produce it. She also explained the fundraiser and it's purpose.

"As you know, all the fur used in the show was synthetic and any additional donations over the ticket price will be used to lobby for the Denver fur ban on the ballot this November."

She also explained where to drop donations, and who to write checks to if necessary.

The audience slowly began to rise and greet the models, including Angie and Jessica. Many filed past the accountant to leave their donations, while Caleb and Michelle captured the action for their film. Eventually all but a couple of the bigger donors had departed, and the maintenance crew began collecting chairs and taking down the curtains.

Caleb gazed into Angie's face thinking, "*I haven't seen her this relaxed in months!*"

Jessica was beaming with happiness as the models gathered around for any further instructions. Each was provided with an application to join Angie and Jessie's burgeoning new agency, and told when to expect their pay.

"Make sure we have your correct contact information before you leave," instructed Angie.

Each model checked the show's roster for accurate contact information, and began to filter out of the room. Finally only Donna, Angie and her small entourage remained.

"I think it went really well," commented Angie.

"You girls did great!:" replied Donna. "The people just loved you!"

"Oh I hope so!" exclaimed Jessica.

"I'll go pull up my truck so we can load up," commented Caleb.

"I'll help you," added Michelle.

"Let's go celebrate in the bar after we get packed up," suggested Jessica.

"I'm in," commented Michelle.

"What do you think Caleb?" asked Angie.

"Sounds good to me!"

Soon the four friends were seated at a table waiting for a server.

Eventually a bubbly brunette arrived at their table and said, "Hi I'm Nicole, and I'll be your server this afternoon. Can I take your order, or is there something you would like to taste first?"

"Can I try your pale ale?" asked Michelle.

"Sure honey, I'll be right back. Would anyone else like to try it?"

All three voiced an affirmative in unison, as the server walked away to get four shot glasses.

"This is good!" exclaimed Jessica.

"Yes, I'll have one of these," added Caleb.

The others all nodded and Nicole went to fill their mugs.

"Did you get a lot of donations?" asked Caleb.

"I think so," replied Angie. "I noticed a lot of checks being written, so I assume that would mean larger amounts than cash gifts."

Michelle added, "I was watching a few of the amounts as they were filling out the checks, and I know I was seeing lots of zeros on the left side of the decimal point!"

"That's awesome guys," said Caleb. "I'm proud of you!"

Michelle added, "I hope it will make a big difference for the animals."

"I'm sure it will," replied Angie.

"So what's next on your agenda?" asked Caleb.

Jessica and Angie looked at each other and shrugged their shoulders in unison.

"I don't know, we haven't had time to think about it!"

"I'm sure you'll be on to your next big project shortly."

"Yeah, we always think of something once we put our minds to it," replied Jessica.

"That we do," said Angie.

Betrayal on Elk Creek

Fall was in the air on a beautiful sunny Rocky Mountain late summer morning. Shadow limped out of the den into a clearing where the early morning sunshine could sooth his shattered hip. He was doing his best to feed his family, but his wound was not healing properly and hunting was becoming more difficult every day. Ember also did what she could, hunting endlessly for small prey near the den to feed her ravenous pups. The young ones were enthusiastically learning to hunt by this time, but lacked the strength and experience to make a significant difference in the pack's food supply.

Eventually Shadow summoned the strength to strike out in search of the day's sustenance. No longer able to chase down swift footed prey such as mule deer and elk, he was forced to rely on his own cunning to outsmart the ranchers and steal what he could from their herd. He slowly limped down the same rocky trail that Caleb had used to gather evidence, when he caught the scent of a freshly killed mule deer. Normally he would avoid a dead carcass in favor of fresh meat killed with his own teeth, but in his weakened condition any kill might make the difference in the survival of his young family.

The dead deer soon came into view, and Shadow approached carefully. The kill might belong to a mountain lion or a bear, and he was in no condition for a fight with a foe more powerful than himself. When it appeared that he was the first carnivore on the scene, he approached more boldly hoping to drag the animal back to his den. As he circled for the final pounce, his front paw was suddenly crushed in the powerful iron jaws of an unknown enemy. Try as he might, he could not free his foot from the terrifying beast.

Shadow twisted, turned and yanked at the chain that would not let go. When escape proved impossible, he attacked the iron jaws of death with his own, until his teeth were broken and mouth bleeding profusely. Eventually exhaustion prevailed and Shadow collapsed onto the blood soaked ground, howling for his mate to come to his assistance. Ember heard his cries and quickly herded her young ones into the den. They understood her stern warning to remain hidden inside, and waited quietly for her return.

Ember followed the cries of her mate, and eventually found him lying exhausted beside the deer carcass. As she approached Shadow, another set of powerful iron jaws savagely bit into her leg as well. With a yelp and a cry, she too was engaged in a death struggle with the same soulless beast that held her beloved mate captive. Just as she was about to tear at the iron jaws with her own teeth, she felt a familiar sharp pain. It was the sting of a tranquilizer dart, a sensation she had experienced many times over during the previous year or two.

Shadow too felt the sting, and gazed into his mate's eyes as he slowly lost consciousness. Rangers quickly emerged from the forest to attend to their beloved wolf pair, but the damage to Shadow's broken body was quite severe. Wildlife employees transported the motionless animals out to the road, where they were locked in cages and loaded onto a truck. Rangers returned to the scene with hounds they hoped would lead them to the den where they could also capture the pups. The den was eventually located and the pups captured, except for one that continued to elude officials for several frustrating days.

Shadow awoke in excruciating pain from his old bullet wound and injuries sustained while attempting to escape from the trap. His eyes slowly focused on his mate, but he was unable to respond with the usual joy he felt when she greeted him. He found only enough strength to lie on his side and whine. She as well soon recovered from the tranquilizer drugs, and heard his whimpers. She tried to reach him, but the steel bars of her enclosure prevented her from getting close enough to lick his wounded face.

Finding himself unable to physically connect with his mate, Shadow drew strength in the depth of her loving eyes of green fire, as the light of life slowly faded from his own. The terrible pain began to slowly subside as the life force drained out of his broken body. Ember soon sensed the departure of his spirit and began to howl in mournful dismay. Rangers eventually discovered Shadow's lifeless carcass when they responded to Ember's cries, but nothing they tried could comfort the grieving matriarch of Colorado's first wolf pack since their extinction in the previous century.

"What do we do?" one of them asked.

"I don't know, I think wolf mates remain at each other's side for a time of mourning until they are ready to move on. Maybe we should cage them together."

Another asked, "Do we have her pups yet? Maybe it would help if we could get her back together with her pups."

"I don't think we have them yet."

"We have to do something."

"We can't tranquilize her again without authorization."

Let's just scoot his cage right up next to hers so she can touch him."

Ember pressed up against Shadow's lifeless body, but her howling continued until wildlife officials could no longer bear it and left her alone to mourn.

Ember was eventually checked over by the veterinary staff and placed in a comfortable facility, but the improved environment did nothing to comfort her broken spirit. For days she refused to eat, unwilling to provide any solace for those who watched over her and cared so deeply for her precious life. Each morning she listlessly greeted her captors with a cold lifeless stare, until one day when she heard the yipping and barking of her nearly forgotten pups. She leaped to her feet as one by one they joyfully entered her enclosure. Ember excitedly licked their faces as they climbed all over her and frolicked together.

"I think we may have found the answer to her sadness," said one employee.

"Yes, it looks like she has finally found a reason to live."

"Maybe she'll eat now."

"I don't know, let's toss some meat in there and see what happens."

Ember eagerly snatched the meat and began to tear off pieces for her pups.

"Look, she's starving and still she cares for her pups first."

"She has a powerful mother's instinct for sure."

As if she could count, she carefully checked them over and began frantically looking around the cage. It soon became clear that she had noticed something was amiss."

"Look, she's searching for the missing pup."

"Yes, she seems to remember that there's another one."

"Oh my God, I hope we catch him soon."

"I hope these four are enough to help mend her spirit... she's such a beautiful soul, we simply can't afford to lose her."

Ember's fifth offspring was eventually captured unharmed. Her broken spirit began to heal, and her reunited family once again bonded as a functioning pack. Her memory of Shadow eventually faded, and she waited patiently with her young ones for the day when they would once again romp joyously and free among the pines beneath the bright Colorado sunshine.

Wolf Quest

Far to the north of Elk Creek, another wolf pack was emerging from their winter shelter. The North Peak Pack was the first wild wolf pack to enter Colorado in many decades. Great excitement gripped Colorado's wildlife watching community, and Caleb was eager to search for them with the hope of a capturing an image to go with a story he was writing about them.

By late spring most of the snow had melted on Colorado's high mountain passes, and Caleb was eager for a road trip. It was still dark when Angie rolled over to put her arm around him, only to find he wasn't there. She arose and went into the kitchen, quickly noticing hot coffee steaming in the pot. Caleb in deep concentration at his desk, was shuffling through a a growing pile of prints he was gathering from the internet. She poured herself a cup of the hot brew and asked, "What are you up to Caleb?"

"Oh, I'm working on a story about the North Peak Pack. I'm trying to figure out if there's any possibility of locating them and getting a picture for my story. Are you up for a road trip?"

"I don't think I'm going to have time. Sorry but Jessie and I are going to be working full time to fill all the orders from the fashion show. I think Michelle has some time off though, maybe she can go with you. I'm sure she would love some time off her job to go adventuring!"

"Of course, I know you got a massive response from the show and that's great!"

Just then Michelle, yawning and rubbing her eyes also entered the room.

"What are we talking about so early in the morning?"

"Caleb wants to go up north and look for the North Peak wolf pack. Don't you have some time off coming?"

"As a matter of fact, I have a two week vacation coming up."

Caleb asked, "What do you have planned?"

"Nothing much, I can't afford to go anywhere. Thought I might go out and see my mom for a couple days."

"Well, how would you like to go up north with me for a few days. It's not that much further to Gardiner from there."

"Caleb be serious, it's half way across Wyoming."

"I know, but we could also go through the Lamar Valley on the way."

"Yeah I guess so, I miss the Lamar."

"Me too., when is your vacation?"

I think the third week in May, but I'll have to check for sure."

"Perfect, the south entrance will still be open for the last week or so of your time off. Is all that okay with you Angie?"

"It think it's a great idea Caleb, Jessie and I are going to be so busy I'll hardly notice."

"Okay then, sound good to you Michelle?"

"It sounds awesome Caleb, only I don't have any money for motel rooms or anything."

"How about we just find some dispersed camping once we get to northern Colorado."

"Works for me!"

Angie commented, "Seems like a great plan, anyway I'm off. Jessie and I are going to meet up at the mall to make plans and make some phone calls, so I'll see you two later."

"And I'm off to work," added Michelle.

"Okay, see you all later. In the meantime I'm going to map out this trip."

Two weeks flew past, and the time for Caleb and Michelle to leave for Elk Creek in northern Colorado was at hand. Michelle was filling her travel mug for her last day of work, and Caleb was grinding coffee for a fresh pot when Angie awoke.

"See you later Angie, I'm off to work!" said Michelle.

"Okay Michelle, have a great day! Aren't you guys leaving tomorrow?"

"We are! I'm all packed and Caleb is going up to RSI this morning for supplies."

"See you later then."

"Do you want to car pool this morning?" Caleb asked Angie.

"I guess you could drop me off at the mall if you want. Jessie and I are supposed to meet in the food court."

"That should work. I can go to the mountain sports store in the mall instead of RSI. They have a lot of the same stuff. That is if you don't mind hitting the grocery store with me on the way home."

"No problem, I don't need to leave for the mall until 9:30 if that's okay."

"Sure, that will give me time to put together a shopping list."

Caleb and Michelle were on the road early the next day, already over Berthoud pass and into Winter Park by lunchtime.

"What do you think about stopping in Winter Park for lunch?" asked Michelle.

"Sounds like a great idea, is Cajun food okay?"

"Cajun is perfect!"

"There's a great little Cajun place here, Jessie and Angie liked it when we were on our way to Craig. Oh and as I told them, they serve you beer in a mason jar."

"Is that a thing?"

"I don't know, probably is down south. I heard it in a country music song, so it must be a thing."

Michelle laughed, "The final verdict, if it's in a country song it has to be true. I'm down for it if you are!"

They were met at the door by the hostess, promptly invited in and seated at a table.

“Will this be okay?” the hostess asked.

“This will be fine,” answered Caleb.

“Can I bring you something to drink?”

“Do you have any Cajun brew on tap?”

“We have a nice pale ale that would go well with a spicy lunch!”

“Sounds good, I'll have one of those.”

“Make it two,” added Michelle.

Soon a waitress returned with the beer, and prepared to take their order.

“What's good?” Michelle asked Caleb.

“I don't know, I always get the blackened catfish, but I'm sure everything is good.”

Michelle looked at the waitress and said, “Make it two blackened catfish then.”

“Well that's easy, two blackened catfish plates coming right up!”

Caleb and Michelle sipped their beer and enjoyed a tasty lunch, while discussing their adventure.

"I wonder if we will really be able to find the wolf pack?" wondered Caleb.

"Well, we could stop in Steamboat and ask the parks office if they have any knowledge of their location. I doubt they would normally give that information out, but they might give it to me."

"That's a great idea Michelle! Hopefully we can just head straight north out of Steamboat to find them, but who knows how far the pack might have roamed by now."

"They should be staying close to their den for a while, at least until the pups get bigger anyway."

They finished their meals and Caleb asked, "Are you ready to hit the road?"

"Yes I am. That was delicious Caleb, thank you!"

"You are certainly welcome! I try to stop in here whenever I get the chance."

The miles rolled by quickly as they always do on the way to an exciting adventure, and the friends soon found themselves rolling into Steamboat Springs.

"I'll GPS the parks office so we don't waste any time."

"Good idea, guide us in!" replied Caleb.

Soon they were parked at the state parks office and Caleb commented, "I don't think I need to go in, why don't you just go ask."

Michelle soon emerged from the building with a big smile on her face. She jumped in the truck and said, “Head straight north out of Steamboat toward Hahn's Peak. The wolves are quite a bit north of there, but there is some dispersed camping up on the Elk River where we can stay two weeks for free.”

“Awesome, let me see if I can find a campsite on my app. We can bring it up on GPS, and should be able to drive right to it.”

Caleb located one of the campgrounds and clicked the start button.

“Okay, this should guide us right to the campground. Better plug into the power though, GPS tracking drains the phone battery fast.”

“Cool, I got it!”

They were already well on their way when Caleb commented, “I know it's 26 miles to Hahn's Peak, because they run a marathon from there to downtown Steamboat Springs every year.”

“Have you ever run it?”

“No, but I think Angie ran it a couple of times before I moved out here.”

The miles passed quickly, and soon road signs indicating their arrival at Hahn's Peak alerted them that smooth pavement would soon give way to dirt roads for the rest of the journey.

“It appears we are going to change over to dirt pretty soon,” commented Michelle.

"Good, it's getting late and I don't want to be looking for the campground in the dark."

Caleb's truck had no problem cruising over the rough dirt terrain, and soon Michelle exclaimed, "We are getting close!"

Caleb slowed and said, "Okay, let me know when the dot is right on the destination."

"Here it is, pull in here!" exclaimed Michelle.

Caleb pulled into the campground and noted, "Looks like we are the only ones here."

"Good, I can't stand being around a bunch of drunks playing loud ass rap music."

"Yeah, me either. I suppose you mostly run into that on the big holidays when the city people all show up in the mountains to party."

Michelle pointed and said, "That looks like a nice spot."

"Yup nice and flat, I think we'll take it."

The pair got out and looked over their surroundings, noticing an approved fire pit with a metal grate.

"We could make a fire, what do you think Caleb?"

"Sure, I'll get the lantern and we can gather some firewood. Let's stick together though, it's dark out here!"

“The moon is almost full, that'll help a bit. I wonder what this full moon is called, is it the Wolf Moon?”

“I don't think so, if I remember correctly this one is the Harvest Moon,” answered Caleb.

“Makes sense, I guess.”

Soon the pair had a nice fire going, and Caleb noticed the glow flickering on Michelle's angelic young face.

“Do you mind if I take your picture? The light of the moon and glow of the campfire look amazing on your face.”

“Sure, I don't mind.”

Caleb retrieved his camera from the truck and dialed in the correct exposure. Not satisfied with his first capture, he moved around the fire and collected a number of different angles.

“There, that should do it,” he commented.

“Cool, can I see them?”

“Of course!”

Caleb turned the LCD screen around so Michelle could see it, and thumbed through the images.

“These are great Caleb, I love them!”

“Yeah, you look amazing tonight!”

"Awww, thanks Caleb," she responded shyly.

Just then, the mournful howl of a distant wolf pierced the darkness.

"Kind of makes the hair on your neck stand up doesn't it," mused Caleb.

"It does, but it's also the most beautiful song I've ever heard."

"It is isn't it? I don't understand why so many are hell bent on silencing it forever."

"Small minded people with small dreams."

"I guess so."

"Caleb, do you think you could teach me photography?"

"Of course, in fact we can start tomorrow if you like. I brought along my backup digital body, along with an old film camera. Maybe we can start you out on the old school film body so you can learn the basics of manual photography."

"Cool, I'd like that. Sitting around in the booth at the park is getting so boring. I don't know how much longer I can stand it."

"I know, I'm not good at boredom either."

"I feel like I'm in prison when you and Angie and Jessie are all having fun and doing exciting things."

"They always want you to model in their shows."

"I know, but I don't really like modeling. I want to be doing what you do."

"Do you want to be a writer too?"

"I don't know, how do I know if I can be a writer?"

"I don't know, I think with writing you either can or you can't."

"How did you know you wanted to be a writer."

"I guess I've been writing stories since I was a little kid. I think writing is hard for most people, a battle to just get words on the page. However with a natural writer it seems like the words are already living inside, fighting to escape."

"Hmm, I don't think that's me. I just want to learn photography."

"Okay, we'll get you set up with some film tomorrow and you can start learning the basics."

"Sounds good, how did you get started?"

"Cameras are another thing I've been interested in since I was a kid. My parents used to let me use an old box camera when we went on vacation."

"How old were you?"

"Probably about ten or twelve. My film budget was one roll of 12 black and white film per year," chuckled Caleb. "I bought my own 110 format camera when I was in high school, and then I took photography in college out in California."

"Is that when you met Lacey?"

"Yes it is, she was in the fashion program at the time."

"How did you meet?"

Michelle detected a distant look in Caleb's eyes as he recounted the story of how he had met his first love in a long distance running class they were enrolled in, to fulfill their physical education requirement at the college."

"We met to run twice a week, five miles up to a reservoir in the mountains."

"Wow!"

Wolf song in the distance subsided and Caleb commented, "Maybe we should douse the fire and get some sleep."

"Yeah, I'm pretty tired."

Caleb offered, "I'll get the fire if you want to lay out the sleeping bags."

"Okay."

Caleb put out the fire being extra careful to stir it, looking intently for any embers that might still be glowing.

Soon he too crawled into the camper topper and slid into his sleeping bag.

"Did you get all the embers?" asked Michelle.

"I did."

"Dang it's cold tonight."

"It sure is, I heard it was going to be in the teens at night here up north."

"Let's zip our sleeping bags together so we can keep each other warm."

Caleb chuckled and said, "Okay, but you will have to try to control yourself."

Michelle laughed, "Shut up!"

The two friends drifted off to sleep in the warmth of each other's body heat, as the sound of night creatures serenaded them under the light of the Harvest Moon.

Wolf Den

Caleb was the first to awaken, eager to get out and start the day. However as he gathered his wits, he discovered himself pinned under Michelle's arm and leg. She was still sleeping soundly, and he wondered how he was going to extricate himself from the sleeping bag without waking her. As he began to slide out of the bedding, she began to stir and was soon fully awake as well.

When she realized their predicament she exclaimed, “Oh my God Caleb, I'm sorry!”

Caleb laughed and replied, “You looked so comfortable, I didn't want to wake you but I need to go!”

“I had no idea I had taken over the whole sleeping bag! Oh my gosh... I need to go too.”

When Caleb finally emerged from the warmth of the cold weather bag he exclaimed, “Dang, it's cold this morning! Where is my coat?”

As they rummaged around for their cold weather clothing Michelle said, “Here's yours on my side.”

“And here's yours on my side. I wonder how that happened?”

Caleb put his coat on and opened the tailgate, letting the crisp autumn air flood their sleeping quarters.

He was the first to exit the truck, and took a deep breath of fresh mountain air. Michelle was right behind him commenting, “What is that you always say, "It doesn't get any better than this!"'"

Caleb chuckled and replied, "I do, but right now I'm wondering why we aren't checking up on tropical wildlife in Hawaii or Tahiti or something!"

"You would hate it there after about a week."

"You are probably right."

"Hey look, we managed to pick a site close to the restrooms."

"Awesome, let's go!"

Soon they were both back at the campsite, and Caleb was fiddling with his GPS tracker.

"What are you doing?"

"I'm feeding the coordinates you got from the state into the GPS unit. We should be able to zero right in on the den, are you ready to go?"

"Are we coming back to this same spot?"

"I don't know, I suppose we'd better not plan on it."

"Okay, let me grab our chairs sand water bottles and I'll be ready."

"I'll warm up the truck while you do that."

Soon they were on their way, following the pointer on Caleb's trail tracker. The road got rougher as they traveled north on Forest Service roads, but that didn't diminish their determination to find the wolf pack.

"You doing okay?" Caleb asked.

"Don't worry about me, just keep going!"

After bouncing around for a couple more hours, Michelle commented, "Looks like we're getting close."

"I hope so, we have to be getting close to Wyoming."

Michelle commented, "I don't know exactly how to tell distance on this thing, but I think we are really close, like right now."

Caleb stopped the truck to look at the display, and then looked around at their current position. There was a rocky hill beside them, and another rugged outcropping just ahead. He turned to Michelle and said, "I'll bet their den is somewhere in that rocky knoll ahead."

"I'll bet you're right. It looks like we would have a decent view from here if we climbed this hill."

"Grab the binoculars and we'll climb up and take a look."

Michelle reached under the seat and snagged Caleb's binoculars and a bottle of water. Caleb shut off the engine and reached for his water bottle and their packs. He rummaged around in his camera bag for the film camera and said, "I'm putting the film camera in your pack."

"Okay cool, thanks Caleb."

They soon reached the summit of the little mountain and found a place to sit in full view of the rugged terrain ahead.

"I guess we just sit and wait. We can trade off looking through the glass if you want to."

Michelle replied, "Sure, we don't want to go up there too close and end up disturbing them. Thank God it's warming up outside!"

"Yes, the sun is actually starting to feel pretty good I hope I don't fall asleep!"

"I'm used to having to stay awake with nothing to do. You'll feel my elbow in your side if you doze off!"

"I'm sure I will," laughed Caleb. "So are you ready to load some film in your camera?"

"Sure, how do I do it?"

"Well, this is an old school SLR camera and it doesn't do anything automatically."

He showed her how to open the back and spool the film onto the reels.

"Now you have to partially wind it onto the spool with the film advance lever," he said, as he pointed to the lever on top of the camera body.

Over the next few minutes he showed her how to attach the long lens, focus, and use all the controls.

"Wow, this is fun Caleb! I wish I had gotten interested earlier."

"I don't know, I guess we all get interested in things when the time is right."

They had been trading off looking through the binoculars for a couple hours when Michelle exclaimed, “Look, one of the adults has come out!”

“There's no way to tell which one it is from this distance. Maybe I can get a shot with my big lens and enlarge the image on the LCD.”

Caleb snapped a picture and displayed it on the screen. One push of the + button enlarged the image by a factor of ten, and as he examined the results he exclaimed “It's the male, probably coming out to hunt.”

“Let me see!”

Caleb flipped the display so that she could see it and she added, “Yep, it's the male alright!”

Soon one of the pups appeared, followed by another and then the adult mother.

“Caleb, the advance lever stopped working.”

“What, let me see it.”

She handed him the camera, and he showed her the little frame counter.

“You are on frame 36, you've already shot the whole roll! I guess we'd better introduce you to the digital camera now. I don't think I can afford your film budget!” he laughed.

“I got excited when I saw the pups.”

"Yeah, I did too. Look, I've already shot over 400 pictures."

Caleb handed her his digital camera body and showed her how to focus, and how to shoot continuously for a series of images in rapid succession.

"Hand me the film camera, and I'll go down to the truck and get the other digital kit for you."

"Okay, thanks Caleb."

In the meantime, the mother called the pups back into the den and the father disappeared into the forest. Caleb eventually returned with the digital camera, and fixings for lunch. They whiled away the day laying on their backs in the warm autumn sunshine, discussing photography and the Colorado wolf project. Eventually the sun dipped low in the sky and Caleb commented, "I guess we'd better make our way back down to the truck."

"Where are we going to camp tonight?"

"I don't see any reason why we can't just stay right where we are, who's going to be around to care?"

"Good point, we haven't seen anyone all day."

They gathered up their gear and trekked back down the hill to the truck.

Michelle commented, "What do we have to eat?"

"I have some freeze dried meals, we just need to boil some water."

Caleb showed her the flavors he had picked up at the mountaineering store, and she picked one she liked.

"Guess I'll have the chili," Caleb commented. "I'll get the propane burner going and some water boiling."

Soon they were enjoying a not meal just as the sun disappeared behind the mountain. When they were finished Michelle commented, "I'm really tired, should we just hit the sack early?"

"I'm exhausted, that sounds like a great idea."

Caleb was the first in bed, followed by Michelle who snuggled up against him and said, "Wow, it's cold this far north, I'm going to need to borrow your body for a while!"

Caleb laughed and said, "No problem, I'm a bit chilly myself!"

Snuggled closely together for warmth, they both drifted off to sleep under the soft light of the moon.

The aroma of fresh coffee wafted into Caleb's nostrils at first light. His eyes opened and he rolled over to see if Michelle was awake, only to find she wasn't there. The tailgate of the truck was open, so he assumed she must have walked over to the bathroom. Thinking that was a pretty good idea, he slid out of the truck himself for the same reason. However as he made his way around the truck, he found Michelle sitting beside the little one burner brewing a pot of coffee in the old school metal percolator.

"Oh Michelle, you are truly an angel!"

She laughed and said, "It's been two days since you've had coffee. I was worried your heart might stop."

"You know me pretty well!"

"How many years did I make your coffee on your way through Gardiner? I brought you back to life from some pretty rough nights in those days."

"You certainly did. This isn't the first time I told you what an angel you are, is it?"

"Nope," she said as she handed him a steaming cup of java in his insulated travel mug.

As they sat in the early morning light sipping hot coffee, Caleb whispered "Michelle, behind you!"

She turned, and to her astonishment the big male wolf was sitting in a clearing just a few yards away, staring at them with great curiosity.

"Caleb, get your camera!"

"He'll run off if we get up. Let's just watch him for a minute."

After a few intense moments the big canine stood and shook the morning dew off of his fur, and disappeared into the forest like a ghost.

"Wow," she said. "That was intense!"

"It was, reminds me of the time I got caught in a blizzard in the Lamar. The wolves were just outside my truck watching over me."

"I wonder if the pups are out?"

"I don't know, grab your digital body and let's climb up and see."

When they got to the summit, the mother and pups were out playing in the morning sunshine.

Michelle commented, "Looks like the daddy wolf must have been on his way out for a hunt when he visited us."

"It appears so, I don't see him anywhere."

The frolicking pups once again entertained the two wildlife enthusiasts for a couple hours, before the mother wolf called them back into the den.

"Did you get some good pictures of the pups today?" Caleb asked.

"I think I did. Should we climb back down the hill and look them over?"

"Sure, it's getting late anyway. We haven't seen the dad return in the light yet."

Michelle commented as they made their way back down the mountainside in the deepening darkness, "Maybe we should make a fire tonight."

"That sounds really nice. There hasn't been a soul drive by here the entire time we have been here, and there are no fire bans as far as I know. Maybe we should pick up some kindling and a couple small logs on our way down."

By the time they arrived at the truck, they had enough wood to get a small fire started.

"I'll get the camp shovel out of the back and dig a fire pit. We can bury it when we're done with it, and nobody will ever know."

Soon the pair was enjoying a warm campfire, and Caleb retrieved a pint of whiskey from his backpack.

"Want a sip?" he asked.

"Sure, I'll try a little."

Caleb handed her the bottle and she took a sip. She closed her eyes as the smooth brew slid down her throat, and then took another sip.

"Oh, you brought the good stuff!"

"Smooth isn't it!"

Caleb took another sip and handed it back to Michelle.

Eventually their conversation died down and Michelle commented, "I feel a little numb!"

"Yeah, me too, I suppose that means we've had enough for one night. I guess we should bury the fire and hit the sack."

The next morning Caleb awoke to Michelle's voice, "Caleb do you have any water left, I have cotton mouth and a headache."

"Always," he replied. "I have some aspirin too, if you would like some."

"Aspirin would be awesome."

She sat up when Caleb handed her the hangover medicine, and noticed her heavy shirt and sweatpants missing.

"Oh my God Caleb, I must have been hot when we went to bed. Do you see my shirt anywhere?"

Caleb laughed, "I don't know, I think I was asleep before my head hit the pillow and I didn't wake up until you talked this morning."

Eventually Caleb noticed her shirt hanging over the tailgate and laughed, "Looks like you didn't make it all the way into the truck with it."

"Dang, I guess I'm not used to drinking!"

"Oh well no worries, it was fun sitting by the fire." replied Caleb.

"It was nice wasn't it?"

The mama wolf and her pups weren't around that day or the next, and the pair debated leaving for Montana.

"I guess we saw them for a while, and we got pictures. Mission accomplished, I suppose!" exclaimed Caleb.

"Maybe we should stay around one more day. We haven't seen the male now for days, I hope he is okay."

"Okay, we'll try again one more time tomorrow morning."

The entire day passed without a sighting of any of the wolves at the den, and the wolf watchers decided they would depart for Montana in the morning.

"We should probably go back down to Steamboat in the morning. I don't know what these roads are like north of the border, and we can take Highway 40 out of Steamboat, all the way to Salt Lake."

"Maybe we should stop in at the parks office and tell them what we discovered."

"That's a good idea."

Caleb and Michelle were in Steamboat at the parks office by mid morning and Michelle said, "Why don't you come in with me this time, they might want to talk to both of us."

As Michelle told the story of the wolf family, a sad countenance overtook the rangers initial friendly demeanor.

"What, what's wrong?" asked Michelle.

"I'm afraid I have some bad news."

"Oh no, what is it?"

"It seems the male ventured over the Wyoming border, and it's been confirmed that he was legally shot and killed by a hunter."

Tears welled up in Michelle's eyes and Caleb exclaimed, "What, seriously?"

"Yes, hunters are waiting across the border for our wolves to cross the boundary where they can kill them on sight."

"Don't they care that they are Colorado's wolves?"

"No, in fact I think they kind of relish any pain they can cause us Colorado wildlife people."

"Can't we sue them for lost revenue or something?"

"No, there's really nothing we can do., especially for a wolf that probably wandered in from Wyoming in the first place."

"Well damn, he was probably on his way up there to hunt when he stopped to check us out the other morning."

Michelle was still unable to speak, and just tearfully nodded. When she regained her composure she commented, "This is just like when Luna was shot in Yellowstone, it was awful."

The three wildlife lovers stood in silence for a full minute before Caleb finally said, "Why don't we get some lunch and head for Wyoming."

Michelle replied, "I don't have much of an appetite, let's just get going."

"Sure," replied Caleb, and they walked to the truck in silence.

The Lamar Valley

Caleb and Michelle drove for miles without speaking a word, and they passed through Craig without stopping. Nearly an hour later, Caleb asked Michelle if she wanted to go into the Sand Wash Horse Management area.

"No, let's just keep going."

"You got it, we can stop in Vernal for gas."

They rode in silence all the way across Colorado, barely speaking at all. The miles and the hours slipped past, hill after sandy hill, mile marker after mile marker. Caleb thought to himself, "*It's strange how the miles pass so quickly when the excitement of a road trip is building, and so slowly when that initial thrill is gone.*"

Michelle's thought's drifted back to her childhood, her mom, and the long years helping out at the cafe in Gardiner. She hadn't been back to Montana since she had left for Colorado several summers before. The long boring winters on the high prairie clouded her memory of the place, and she wondered how her mother had been able to tolerate such emptiness all those years. She worried what grief her own absence may have visited upon her, and what it would be like to see her face after such a lone period of time.

Finally Caleb broke the silence, "We are almost to Utah."

"Good, I need a restroom break."

"Me too, should we stop there and eat too?"

"No, I still don't have much of an appetite."

"Okay, we'll just grab some snacks for the road then. I think we can make it to Jackson before nightfall if we hustle."

"That's good Caleb, I don't think I feel like camping tonight. Can we get a hotel room?"

"Sure, it would be nice to get a shower and sleep in a soft bed."

Soon the pair was back on the road and Michelle became a little more talkative, "It will be nice to see the Tetons again."

"They are magnificent aren't they," agreed Caleb.

"What is wrong with those hunters that they don't care how much pain they cause."

"I don't know, selfishness, dead in their souls. How they can get a thrill from watching a beautiful creature fall to the ground dead is beyond me."

"I hate them."

"Me too., I wish we could get the western wolves back on the endangered list. I don't know how they can say they aren't endangered, when every half wit in Wyoming and Montana with a gun is out to kill every one they find, including that moron of a governor."

Once again, silence became the theme and darkness began to fall on the barren Wyoming countryside.

"Are we almost to Jackson?" Michelle asked.

"Maybe an hour to go."

"Good, this has been an awfully long ride."

"Yes it has."

Eventually they rolled into Jackson and spotted a vacancy sign. Michelle noticed it first, and said, "That looks like a nice place Caleb."

"It is a nice place. That's where Angie and I stayed on our way home after the wedding."

"Oh Caleb, let's find another place. This one has romantic memories for you."

"It's no big deal, it's a nice place. Let's just stop."

"But what will Angie think?"

"Good point, I don't want to step into that mine field. Keep an eye out for the next one."

"Here, this one says vacancy too, and it's a plain old ordinary travel style motel, nothing romantic."

"Perfect," Caleb said as he pulled into the parking lot. "I'll go check us in. Should we get a double or a single?"

"Just get a single, there's no sense wasting money."

Caleb soon returned with the keys and Michelle asked, "Should we order a pizza?"

"That would be awesome Michelle, and we still have some beer in the cooler."

With their bellies full of food, the travelers were soon ready for a good night's sleep.

"Do we want to get an early start in the morning?" asked Caleb.

"Sure," replied Michelle. "The sunrise on the Tetons will be awesome, and I would like to get up to my old beat in the Lamar Valley as soon a possible."

"That's right, that was your beat when you were with the National Park Service. I guess it was kind of my beat too, as a writer for the Bozeman newspaper."

"Do you want to go back to Bozeman on this trip?"

"No, I don't miss it."

Caleb awoke to the aroma of fresh coffee. As he began to stir Michelle said, "Look Caleb, they have a little coffee pot!"

"That's great, I really need a cup."

She poured the steaming brew into one of the paper cups and handed it to Caleb. She also poured one for herself and sat down at the little table.

"I don't think we are going to have enough to fill our travel mugs."

"No worries, we need to get gas somewhere and I'm sure they will have coffee for the road."

Soon they were back on the road, cruising north as the morning sun illuminated the spectacular peaks of the Grand Teton mountain range.

"I saw a moose here one time when I was on my way through."

"I hope we see one today, that would be amazing!" replied Michelle.

"Why don't you get your camera ready just in case."

"Oh right, I guess I'm not thinking like a photographer yet!"

Caleb laughed, "Give it time, you will eventually have a camera with you all the time."

There were no moose along the highway this time, and the pair passed by many familiar tourist spots on their journey to the north end of the park, Both had seen the sights before, and had their minds set on reaching the Lamar Valley before dark.

"Look Caleb, Tower Junction is only twenty more miles."

"Great, should we stop and have a late lunch at the lodge?"

"We should, I used to stop there once in a while when I was on my way home from work and I have a lot of nice memories there. I wonder if any of my old friends are still working there?"

"I don't know, I guess we are about to find out!"

Indeed, Michelle's old high school friend Brittany was now managing the restaurant, and she immediately recognized Michelle.

"Michelle,' she exclaimed, "It has been so long, where have you been?"

"I moved to Colorado a couple years ago, I guess I didn't get the chance to tell everyone before I left. It was kind of a whirlwind at the time."

"And who is this handsome man, is this your husband?"

Michelle laughed, "No this is my bud Caleb, maybe you remember him from when he was a reporter in Bozeman. He spent a lot of time here in the Lamar reporting on the wildlife."

"Nope, can't say I do. What are you doing back here?"

"Oh we are just visiting, on our way to see my mom up in Gardiner for a couple of days."

"I remember your mom, didn't she run the coffee shop where you worked?"

"She sure did, still does as a matter of fact!"

"Well come on in and have a seat, I'll have a server come and take your order."

Brittany was soon busy with a large group, and Caleb and Michelle quietly finished their meal. Michelle bid her old friend farewell and they were soon back on the road, descending into the beautiful Lamar Valley.

"I have so missed this place," commented Caleb.

"Isn't it beautiful?" replied Michelle.

"I hope we get to see some wolves today."

"Wouldn't that be amazing?"

As they slowly cruised along the Lamar River, a traffic jam began to form ahead of them.

"Wolf jam I bet," mused Caleb.

"Yup, you can pretty much guarantee it," replied Michelle. "Let's find a parking place and check it out."

"Okay grab the cameras."

As they strode toward the growing crowd on top of a nearby bluff, Michelle began asking what was going on. Finally someone in the know commented, "It's the Junction Butte Pack, 1478 and 1479 are putting on a show!"

"Awesome," replied Michelle.

Two young wolves were at play just across the river, as the rest of the Junction Butte Pack looked on from further away. Someone standing nearby said, "It's 1478 and 1479, two young females that have grown up along the river. They are quite used to people, and aren't afraid to come close."

Michelle and Caleb watched as the two wolves frolicked, chasing each other around and play fighting.

"How old are they?" asked Caleb.

"They are about two years old, maybe a little more."

"Wow, this is amazing, almost seems like they know the people are watching them!"

"I think they are aware that they are the stars of the show."

Eventually the two young wolves returned to the pack, and they all disappeared together into the forest across the vast valley to the south.

"Wow, that was more than I ever expected to see here today!" commented an elated Caleb.

"No, that was incredible. Usually people just have to be content to watch them in the distance with spotting scopes. Did you get any good pictures?"

"I think so, how about you?"

"I don't know, I can't tell yet whether I'm getting anything good or not."

"I'm sure you did fine, as you gain experience you'll know right away," replied Caleb. "What do you think, do you want to go on up to Gardiner, or should we camp out somewhere tonight."

"Let's camp, I would love to hear the packs howling tonight."

"Okay, let's go see if we can find a campsite at Slough Creek."

"Works for me," replied Michelle.

They were set up for a night along Slough Creek by nightfall, with a nice fire going in the grated pit. Caleb leaned back on a rock and took a swig of the smooth whiskey they had tried on their previous camping trip in northern Colorado. Michelle squeezed in close, using Caleb as a pillow. He felt her shiver and handed her the whiskey, as he wrapped his arms around her. He chuckled as she took her first sip and reminded her, "Be careful, this is the stuff that makes your shirt fall off!"

She laughed, “Maybe I should just stick to a couple sips this time.”

Caleb stared up at the stars as Michelle became mesmerized by the flickering flames of the campfire. They could hear wolf packs howling at each other from opposite sides of the valley and Michelle commented, “Probably the Mollies.”

“Yup, they are warning each other to stay on their own side of the valley.”

Michelle also looked up at the stars and said, “Isn't this amazing, I wish this moment would never end.”

“Me too, I have missed this place so. Right here right now, it's like the rest of the world doesn't matter, or even exist.”

The two sat in silence in the warmth of the fire, until the flames sputtered out and the glowing coals grew dark.

Home in Montana

Caleb was awake before sunrise, and was heating water when Michelle emerged from the camper topper. "Whatcha doing?" she asked.

"Just heating up some water for the coffee."

"Wow, wasn't last night just like a dream?"

"I don't know how it could be anything else here. I think this is my favorite place on earth."

"Me too, but I still wouldn't want to come back and live here. I love our beautiful home in Colorado, with you and Angie."

"Yeah, it's pretty incredible isn't it. Getting the house in Franktown was well worth Angie moving away from Bozeman for a career in real estate."

"I just love living with you guys."

"Awww, we like having you there too."

As they swallowed the last of their coffee Caleb said, "What do you think, should we head back down to the river for a while?"

"Sure, I'm not in a big hurry to get up to Gardiner."

The wolves were resting in the sunshine on the opposite side of the valley when Caleb and Michelle arrived at the little overlook. A few spotters were already set up in their lawn chairs looking through powerful telescopes.

Caleb asked, “Anything going on today?”

“No, the pack is pretty quiet this morning.”

Michelle noticed a group gathering around a ranger at the bottom of the hill. She recognized her old friend April from the park service years before, and nudged Caleb to follow her down the hill. Caleb acknowledged the nudge and looked over, quickly recognizing April himself.

“Hi April, how are you doing?” exclaimed Michelle.

“Michelle, long time no see! Are you coming back to work?”

“No, Caleb and I are just out to visit my mom for a little bit.”

“Hi Caleb, haven't seen you in a while either! Michelle, are you still living in Colorado too?”

“Yes, I work for the sate parks department on the Front Range,” replied Michelle.

“Cool, too bad about the Elk Creek Pack, huh.”

“What, what about the Elk Creek Pack?”

“Oh, you didn't hear?”

“No, I've been on vacation for a little bit.”

“Oh yeah, after a few cattle depredations they decided to relocate the pack. It turns out that the breeding male was badly injured and died during medical treatment.”

Caleb and Michelle stood in stunned silence. After a while Caleb said, “I saw the male a little while ago. I'm pretty sure he had a bullet in his hind quarters, shot by a rancher in the area. I did a story on the whole thing.”

“What about the rest of the pack?” asked Michelle.

“They are all being kept together while they figure out what to do.”

“Oh my God, I knew something like this was going to happen eventually, Well, we'd better let you get back to work, it was great seeing you again April!”

“Nice to see you too!, say hi to your mom for me, and nice to see you too Caleb.”

“Wow, this isn't a good week for the wolves is it?”

Caleb replied, “No, you know I just saw Shadow a couple of weeks ago. He was limping, but he certainly didn't look like he was near death. There has to be something Colorado isn't admitting. Something bad must have happened in the capture.”

“I wonder if they will tell me, after all I was on the release team. If they hurt those wolves it's going to be really hard going back to work for them. I might quit if they won't tell me what happened.”

“You don't like working in that stupid hut anyway. Why don't you demand a better higher paying position. Then if they won't give it to you, turn in your notice.”

“But what would I do for a living?”

"I don't know for sure, but I have an idea. I have way too much work to do with all the little research trips and all the writing, plus the books. I could really use an assistant."

"Oh Caleb, that would be so amazing!"

"I have to clear it with Angie first though, so don't say anything to her until I have a chance to talk to her first."

"Okay, I won't say anything."

Caleb looked up at the sun and said, "Looks like it's getting on in the morning. We probably won't see any more wildlife today, should we just head for Gardiner?"

"Yeah, I just really wanted to camp in the valley last night, wasn't it awesome?"

"Yes, one of the best camp outs I've ever been on!

The last of the lunch crowd was clearing out of the cafe when they turned into the parking lot. Michelle got out and headed for the door as Caleb fumbled around looking for his wallet. His head snapped around when he heard a scream at the front door of the cafe, as Michelle's mom Julie came running out to greet her. Caleb watched with a smile on his face as his young friend greeted her mother, after over a year of absence. After a bit, he too walked over to greet his old friend, one who had treated him so kindly when he was first establishing his business in the region.

"Caleb, how are you, It has been so long!"

"It has been a long time!" replied Caleb as he reached out for a hug.

Julie squeezed him hard for several seconds and then invited the travelers inside.

"Well come on in, let's sit down and get caught up!"

"Hey Jennifer, can you bring us all a cup of coffee?" she asked her young hostess.

"Sure Julie, who are your new friends?"

Julie introduced Michelle first, "This is my daughter Michelle, Michelle this is Jennifer, she has your old job."

Jennifer held out her hand to greet Michelle, and Julie introduced Caleb. "This is my old friend Caleb, he's a famous author and photographer."

"Well I don't now about famous," smiled Caleb.

All three sat down at Caleb's favorite table, as Michelle excitedly told her mom all about her adventures in the big city.

The two women were totally engrossed in their conversation while Caleb caught up with the news and his messages on the phone. As they all relaxed, Caleb's thoughts turned to Angie and he sent out a quick message, "Hi Angie, we made it to Gardiner. We are sitting in the coffee shop right now, and Michelle and Julie are getting all caught up on lost time!"

"That's good Caleb, how was the drive?"

"It was long, but we got to spend some time in the Lamar Valley today. We got to see the Junction Butte Pack, and the two young wolves

1478F and 1479F put on quite a show."

"Oh that's great, what were they doing?"

"Well they seem quite used to the rows of scopes up by the road, and were playing just on the other side of the river."

"Oh, did you get some good pictures?"

"I think so, haven't had time to really look at them yet."

"Did you hear about the Elk Creek Pack?"

"Yes we just did, isn't that sad?"

"I know... a lot of people are really upset here on the front range."

"Yeah, Michelle is devastated. She wants to quit the park's service."

"What would she do?"

"Well, I told her I would have to check with you, but I was thinking I could sure use an assistant."

"That's a great idea Caleb, then you would have more time to help me and Jessie!"

Caleb laughed, "I suppose I would, but I was thinking I would have more time for writing, if I had someone to help with the research."

"Oh I know, I was just kidding."

"No, I would love to help out with your business as well, it's no problem! Anyway, Michelle will be excited to hear that she doesn't have to spend every day staring at the walls in the park kiosk."

Angie replied, "I don't know how she has lasted this long."

"Okay, I'll let her know."

Angie replied, "Okay, well I'd better get back to it. We have a meeting tomorrow about another show. Our faux fur show was such a success that they want us for something else. We'll find out tomorrow."

"Okay Angie, sounds exciting. Call me after your meeting and let me know all about it!"

The group eventually departed the cafe and reconvened at the old house. Julie went into the back room and walked out of the hallway with an armload of pillows and blankets. As she dropped them on the couch she said, "I kept Michelle's room set up for her hoping she would come back and visit me sometime, so she can sleep there. I thought you could sleep on the couch, if that's okay with you."

"The couch will be just fine."

"Okay, I have to be up by four in the morning to open up the cafe, so I'm going to get to bed."

"That's fine, we are pretty tired ourselves. It's been a long few days," he replied.

"Yeah, I can't wait to get into my soft bed!" replied Michelle.

All three were sound asleep in short order.

Caleb was already wandering around with his flashlight in the morning, trying to find coffee when Julie's alarm went off. She walked in, turned on the light and said, “Oh I'm sorry to wake you Caleb.”

“No worries, I was already awake. In fact I was about to look for the coffee.”

Julie laughed, “I should have remembered, you need your coffee!”

“Yeah, I wish I had a dollar for every cup of coffee you served me at the cafe, on my way back and forth to and from Yellowstone.”

“We do go back a ways!”

“How has business been?”

“It was tough getting through the pandemic, but the tourists are finally starting to return. Of course my regulars weren't about to let a little virus keep them away.”

“I can't imagine masks being too popular in Gardiner either.”

“Nobody in this town got rich selling masks, I can tell you that for sure,” she laughed.

Caleb chuckled, “No, I imagine not.”

“Well I gotta run Caleb. The coffee and filters are in the overhead cabinet, and you are welcome to make all you want!”

“Okay, have a nice day. We'll probably stop in for lunch if that's okay.”

"I'm looking forward to it!"

Julie departed and Caleb turned on the TV to watch the morning local news, and was startled by a heading that flashed across the screen, *Tragedy in Yellowstone.*

Caleb imagined someone was killed by a bison, or drowned in the river or something, but nothing could have prepared him for the devastating story that followed. A grim faced reporter recounted events from the night before, when beloved grizzly 399 had been hit by a car and killed. Female grizzly 399 had been a Yellowstone favorite for seventeen years delighting tourists and locals alike, as she raised many cubs to adulthood. Now she was gone, and her young cub Spirit was nowhere to be found. Soon social media was also lighting up with the news, with thousands of grief stricken comments on the park service news post regarding the incident.

Tears welled up in Caleb's eyes when Michelle walked into the kitchen and he had to break the news, "I have some really bad news."

"What Caleb, what's wrong, is my mom okay?"

"Oh no, it's not that. I just saw on the news that 399 was killed by a car on the highway last night."

"Oh my God, she said as she burst into tears. "This is just too much, I can't stand it anymore."

Caleb knew there was no point in saying any more, or even trying to comfort her with a hug. Tears would just have to fall, along with the thousands of others who had loved 399 through the years.

The Election

Caleb was banging away at his keyboard when Angie returned from running errands.

"Did you go vote today?" she asked.

"No not yet, not sure I see the point."

"What do you mean?"

"None of the politicians are going to do what they say, and if one does happen to do something, it will only make things worse. The current administration has done nothing to protect wildlife, in fact they sued to continue the worst of the wildlife policies from the previous administration."

"That's true I guess."

"And, even if one party would carry through with promises I approve of, both parties are pushing policies I abhor. How can I vote for someone that I'm positive is going to absolutely stomp all over my conscience?"

"Well, at least go in and check the boxes for voter initiatives you want to see passed. At least go in and vote for the fur ban even if you do nothing else."

"I guess that makes sense, have you gone yet?"

"No, I was going to wait for Michelle to get home, and we are going to go together."

"I might as well go along too."

"Cool, thanks Caleb. I wouldn't feel right if you didn't at least honor all the work we did putting on the show."

"You are right, I wouldn't feel right either. With my luck, I'd find out tomorrow that the fur ban needed one more vote to pass, and I was to blame."

Angie laughed, "You would be sleeping in the garage until the next election."

Caleb chuckled, "I believe you!"

Angie looked up as she heard the muffled sound of a car door closing out in the driveway.

"That's probably Michelle."

Caleb looked at his watch and said, "Yup, it's about that time. I'll go get dressed."

"Hurry, we don't have a lot of time before the polls close."

"Okay, just take me a second."

Michelle walked in and said, "Any news about the election returns yet?"

Angie replied, "No, they aren't allowed to talk about it until the polls closed."

Caleb walked back into the room and said, "I remember one election out in California, where the presidential election was already called before most of California even got to vote."

Let's get going," urged Angie.

"I just need to use the bathroom real quick," commented Michelle.

Soon the trio was on their way to their assigned polling location.

"Who are you going to vote for Caleb?" asked Michelle.

"I don't know, I'm kicking around the idea of leaving all the candidates blank and just voting for the initiatives. Oh, and of course I always vote no on all the judges. I just assume they are all crooked and put "do not retain" on all of them."

"What if one of them is a good judge?" asked Angie.

"Do you know of one? If you know a good one I'll vote to keep them."

"Well now that you mention it, I guess I don't."

"Have any cases gone our way this year?"

"Well no, I guess not."

"I rest my case."

Michelle laughed, "The world according to Caleb."

Angie laughed too, "He does have his own way of thinking about things."

The parking lot was already half full by the time they arrived and Angie said, "What happens if the poll closes before we get to vote?"

Caleb replied, “I don't know, I think maybe you still get to vote if you are already inside when they close the doors.”

“I hope so,” added Michelle.

The trio was greeted by a smiling poll worker as they entered the room. One woman scurried over when she recognized Angie, and reached out for a hug.

“Laura!” exclaimed Angie. “It's been a long time, how are you?”

“Oh I'm fine, how are you doing? I was at the mall when you were all putting on that fashion show!”

“You should have come over and said hello!”

“You all looked so busy, I thought I'd stop by after the show but it went on long.”

“It was a crazy day, that's for sure!”

Next she turned to Michelle, “Hi Michelle! Bob said you were at the gate today when he came through to go fishing.”

“Yes, it was one of my days to watch the entrance.”

Laura led the three friends over to the voting booths and showed them where to drop their completed ballots. Soon they were finished voting, and each one dropped their selections into the box.

“That went really fast!” exclaimed Angie.

“Yeah, not too bad,” replied Michelle.

"Look, Caleb is still voting. He looks like he is being forced to swallow a lemon," commented Angie

"Basically he is, isn't he?"

"Yeah, he's a man of complex convictions."

Caleb dropped his ballot into the box and walked over.

"You don't look like you enjoyed yourself much," commented Angie.

"No, it would be a lot easier if they weren't all hell bent on destroying the country and the state."

"Yeah, they all seem like they are just in it for the money."

"Bunch of lawyers, what do you expect."

Angie asked, "Should we go out to dinner somewhere?"

"Sure," exclaimed Michelle. "I'm hungry!"

Caleb replied, "I didn't see a whole lot of cars at the Stage Line, should we go there?"

"Sounds good to me," replied Michelle.

Hopefully we won't get into a fight this time!" mumbled Angie.

"We've been there a million times, and there was just that one time."

"True," replied Angie.

Soon they were all seated at a table with drinks while they waited for their food orders.

"I sure hope the fur ban passes." commented Angie.

Caleb replied, "Me too, but the hunting lobby spent an awful lot of money."

"Yeah, they pulled out all the stops."

"Either way, we are not going to give up," replied Michelle. "Have you seen all the hateful posts about Shadow, how they wished he could have died a more horrible death?"

"No, what are they saying?" asked Angie

"Every vile thing you can imagine. One photographer posted a picture of a wolf from Yellowstone, and the wolf haters even piled in on him. One of their favorite ignorant phrases is "Smoke a pack a day.""

"That's just dumb," replied Angie.

"Ignorant is what it is," replied Caleb. "I heard the ranchers paid for an AI bot to generate anti wolf comments and based on the widespread repetition, I believe it to be true. Plus you can reply to the comments with the most insulting comments you can think of, and all they do is answer with an infuriating smiley face."

"What good do they think that is going to do them?" asked Angie.

"I don't know, but it's not working. In fact all it is doing is causing the majority of voters to hate ranchers. I'll tell you what, I would have voted them off their land today if that was an option."

"Well, maybe we can get some more things on the ballot in two years. If we are persistent I think we will eventually prevail."

"I hope so."

One of Michelle's favorite songs started to play on the Jukebox and she grabbed Angie's hand, "Come on Angie, let's dance!"

Angie started to get up and said, "Come on Caleb, come and join us. You never have any fun anymore."

Caleb thought for a second and stood up, "I don't know if I even remember how to dance."

"It's like riding a bike, you never forget it!"

"Okay, but don't laugh at me."

"Nobody is going to laugh at you."

Caleb took a few steps, and was soon mixing it up on the floor with the girls. Michelle continued to put quarters in the jukebox and the trio laughed and enjoyed themselves until late. Eventually someone else managed to slip in a coin, and a slow song began to play. It was a song very familiar to Angie and Caleb, and he reached out to pull her in close.

Michelle said, "You two love birds have fun, I'm going to the restroom."

The song was over when she returned and Angie said, "Maybe we should hit the road."

The three walked out in silence and got in the car to go home.

"That was fun," Michelle exclaimed.

"It was," replied Angie. "We haven't been out in a long time. Aren't we out kind of late for you though?"

"Today was my last day," Michelle quietly replied.

"What, you finally quit the forest service?"

"I did... I just can't stand sitting in that booth anymore, watching the world go by without me."

"That has to be so miserable," commented Angie. "Didn't you put in for a better position?"

"I did, but it's always the same. Not yet, budget cuts and all that."

Caleb chimed in, "Well that's good news for me. I have more to do than I have time in a day."

Michelle laughed, "So I don't even get one day to be unemployed?"

Caleb chuckled, "You're unemployed tonight. Tomorrow we hit the ground running!"

Michelle smiled, "Honestly I don't know what I would do with a whole day off anyway."

"We're going up to Jefferson tomorrow., I heard they were seeing a lot of moose along the creek. I'll buy you lunch, how about that?"

"It sounds like fun Caleb, do I get to shoot too?"

"That digital camera you used up north is yours now! You can shoot anything you want with it, anytime you feel like it. In fact, you should start carrying it with you so you are ready if something comes up."

"Cool, I'll definitely do that Caleb!"

"Good, you need to program your mind to be a journalist."

"What if I can't write?"

"Well, we'll cross that bridge when we come to it. Just work on your photography skills at this point."

"Okay, thanks Caleb."

Angie interrupted, "Hey, they are starting to report the returns!"

Caleb and Michelle leaned forward to read the results streaming across the screen.

"Look, that reporter looks like someone killed her dog," commented Caleb.

"She does, Turner must have won again."

"I wonder how long it will be before he tries to de-list wolves again?"

"I don't know, I hope he's too busy fixing the economy to get around to destroying the environment and killing the wildlife."

"We can only hope," added Michelle.

"Hey look, they are listing the Colorado results. I wonder if the fur ban passed?"

Caleb answered, "I don't know, I wonder if the results are on the internet?"

Michelle was already thumbing through the results on her phone when her expression turned dark, and she said, "Looks like it failed."

"What?" exclaimed Angie.

"They are saying the media blitz by the ranchers and hunters tipped the scales against us. It has failed to pass."

"Well damn," commented Angie. "This night has sure turned to crap."

Caleb stared at the screen in silence as imagined the carnage the next four years would bring. After a long while he commented, "Mark my words, they will be lobbying to hunt wolves and grizzlies inside the park at Yellowstone, and Turner will probably let them."

"At least we retained the governorship in Colorado.," added Angie.

"Yeah, the wolves will remain protected here in Colorado for the next few years anyway."

Winter Wonderland

Clear mountain air and unbridled joy greeted Ember on a late December morning as her pups romped exuberantly in a foot of fresh powder. The memory of Shadow had faded somewhat, and the pack had grown accustomed to their enclosure. Ember had done the best she could in captivity, to teach her young family to fend for itself. She lay contentedly in the brilliant sunshine and watched her offspring play in the snow. A truck approached, but the family had also grown accustomed to their human benefactors, and paid little attention to their arrival.

The young ones continued to play, but Ember instinctively positioned herself between the humans and her offspring. Suddenly she felt the sting of a tranquilize dart and barked out a warning to her pups. Misunderstanding her command, the young ones stopped playing and came to her aid. Soon they were all lying unconscious in the snow, completely at the mercy of the humans. Once again, the pack was loaded up and ripped from their lives of comfort and safety.

The smell of fresh pine reached Ember's nostrils, and she quickly looked around for her pups. She soon discovered them lying on the snow next to her, slowly regaining consciousness along with her. Soon they were all on their feet, whining nervously from fear and uncertainty. Humans gathered around, speaking and laughing excitedly.

"Seems like they are all waking up okay."

"Yes," said another. I think we can release them any time now."

"Let's give them a few more minutes, so we can send them off with a little nourishment for their first day or two."

A few more minutes passed and each wolf was given a piece of meat, but their fear overcame their appetite and the food lay on the ground uneaten.

"I guess they are too nervous to eat."

"Too bad, they are going to need it. They haven't had to hunt for themselves in a long time."

"I sure hope they can adapt to the wilderness again."

"I think they will."

"Okay, let's release them."

The cages were opened and the confused animals walked out into the open. Now accustomed to humans, they felt no need to flee and slowly meandered into the forest together.

On the other side of the state Angie was up early as well, sorting Christmas decorations and getting a turkey ready for the oven. A bleary eyed Caleb stumbled into the room and poured a cup of coffee.

"Merry Christmas Caleb!"

"Merry Christmas to you too! Hey look, it snowed!"

"Isn't it beautiful?" replied Angie.

Michelle had slipped into the room behind them, noticing the snow as well, "Hey, it snowed last night!"

"Merry Christmas," Angie and Caleb exclaimed simultaneously.

"Oh my gosh, it is Christmas isn't it! Are there parades or something we can watch?"

"I don't know, I guess so. Turn on the TV and see!"

Michelle asked, "Is Jessie coming over today?"

"We didn't make plans, but I'd be surprised if she didn't stop by. She doesn't have much patience for her husband's football buddies," commented Angie.

"No she doesn't," laughed Caleb. "My bet is she's here before lunch."

"We need to have these decorations up before she gets here. I should have had them up long ago, but we have been so dang busy!"

"I'll help!" Michelle eagerly exclaimed and she scurried over to the table where Angie was doing the sorting.

"Can you untangle these lights?"

"Sure, give me the hard job."

Angie laughed, "Oh, they aren't that bad this year. Caleb, why don't you help her out."

Soon Caleb was plugging in strands of lights, and Michelle was testing to make sure they were all working.

Caleb offered to hang the strands and Michelle brought over a box of bulbs. Soon the tree was gleaming with Christmas cheer and the trio sat down to admire their handy work.

"Isn't it beautiful?" exclaimed Angie.

"It is beautiful, it's going to be a wonderful day."

Just then the doorbell rang, and Michelle exclaimed, "Jessie!"

Angie laughed, "Who bet on the time?"

"We didn't make an official bet," commented Caleb,.

Angie went to answer the door and to no one's surprise, in walked a beaming Jessica, "Merry Christmas everyone!"

Both Caleb and Michelle greeted her with an enthusiastic, "Merry Christmas Jessie!"

"I brought wine, who wants some?"

"It's only ten in the morning," replied Angie.

"So what, it's Christmas!"

Michelle laughed, "What the heck, I'll have a glass."

"I don't want to be a party pooper," added Caleb.

Angie poured four glasses of wine while Jessica made herself comfortable on the couch.

"What are we watching?"

Michelle replied, "The Christmas parades of course. Caleb is watching his phone."

"Holy crap, check this out!" he exclaimed.

"What?" asked Michelle.

"They have released the Elk Creek Pack again."

"Seriously? I'm surprised, I didn't know anything about it."

"I don't know Michelle, you've been gone quite a while, maybe you aren't in the loop anymore."

"Maybe not, did they say where?"

"Pitkin County is all it says."

"That's some seriously rugged country, the pack shouldn't bother anyone out there."

"Unless they start eating skiers," joked Jessica.

"I don't think wolves have killed any people since the middle ages. I imagine they will stay clear of Aspen."

Michelle asked, "Are there any ranches in those mountains?"

Caleb swiped his finger across his phone and replied, "Looks like a few, maybe some dude ranches or something."

"Oh, well hopefully they will stay away this time. They've been in captivity a long time, I wonder if they will be able to fend for themselves."

Angie replied, “I don't know how well they will do without Shadow. He was the provider and they killed him.”

“My God look at this hate,” commented Caleb.

“What hate?” asked Angie.

“I'm looking at the comments on this post about the release. It's nothing but hate for the wolves. “Smoke a pack a day, shoot shovel and shut up, let's go hunting boys, over and over. Don't they know it's illegal to kill them?”

“Bunch of morons,” commented Michelle. “We got nothing but threats and hate when we were getting ready to release them the first time.”

“They are a bunch of dumb hillbillies, they can't spell, can't write, can't even string an intelligent sentence together.”

“I hope the rest of the country doesn't think Coloradans are all illiterate,” mused Jessica.

“Oh, there are a few pro wolf comments, and a lot of people ripping into the ranchers. It's a regular internet flame war,” commented Caleb.

Michelle added, “Maybe they have finally learned to stay away from people and cattle, I hope anyway.”

Angie replied, “I think as long as they can find food they will be smart enough to keep to themselves, as long as the ranchers don't deliberately try to bait them and trap them.”

“I wouldn't trust those ignorant fools any further than I can throw them,” replied Caleb.

"I wouldn't put anything past those inbred creeps," replied Angie.

"Me either," added Michelle.

Soon Angie had all the food in the oven, and sat down on the couch next to Caleb to watch the parade and said, "Can you believe the year is almost over?"

Jessica replied, "I know right? Fall just blew past and I didn't even get to go look at the leaves this year."

Angie replied, "Come to think of it I didn't either. We didn't even go to a single Oktoberfest. We always go to at least one festival."

Caleb replied, "Michelle and I saw leaves, but we really didn't have much time to think about it, with all the wildlife incidents going on."

After a few seconds of contemplation, Angie thoughtfully suggested, "We should have a little New Year's Eve party here at the house this year."

"That's a great idea," replied Jessica. "I used to enjoy the little holiday parties that the agency used to throw, back before the pandemic."

Angie added, "Yeah, nothing has returned to normal after that. I don't think we need to have a big party, but maybe we could invite the models that joined us after the fashion show. Maybe it would help them to feel like they belong to something special."

"I know it would mean a lot to me if I were a new person," commented Jessica.

Caleb spoke up, “It's okay with me, let's make it happen!”

Michelle laughed, “Am I invited?”

“Of course honey,” replied Angie. “You are family.”

“Awww, thank you Angie.”

As the little group enjoyed a beautiful Christmas, life for Ember's pack had turned into a desperate fight for survival. Although healthy from medical attention and a steady diet, Ember's leg muscles had atrophied and her pups never had the opportunity to learn to pursue live prey from Shadow. Wolves often travel fifty miles in a day, and the weakened animals struggled in the deep snow to cover just a few.

Unable to take down deer and elk in the harsh mountain environment, they were forced to live on a diet of rabbits and other small game that they could hear scurrying around beneath the deep snow. Eventually the struggling pack found their way into the Crystal River valley, where they were able to find shelter and abundant prey in the tall grass along the banks of the natural waterway.

Canadian Wolves

Caleb and Angie were already sipping coffee at the dining room table when Michelle walked in and took a cup out of the cabinet.

“Aren't you going snowshoeing this morning Caleb?” she asked.

“Maybe in a while. It's too dang cold this morning.”

“What's the temp?”

“Twelve below zero,” Caleb replied.

“Wow, that is cold!”

Michelle took a sip of hot coffee and checked her phone messages. Her eyes lit up when she saw a text from her friend Heather.

“Heather says they are going to be doing another wolf release pretty soon. Apparently they have been preparing a batch for release that they brought down from British Columbia.”

“Cool,” replied Caleb. “Any chance we'll be invited to this release?”

“No, I don't imagine they will be allowing any civilians.”

“I figured.”

“If I had gotten to be involved with the program all along, I'd probably still be working for the parks service.”

Angie replied, "I still don't understand why they wouldn't let you move on from that awful gate job."

"Yeah, me either, I had high hopes for that job when I accepted it. I wonder what it would have been like if I'd just transferred to Colorado with the national parks service."

"Well... I doubt would be living here with us," replied Caleb. "And you wouldn't be working with me."

"No I guess not. All in all the move to Colorado has worked out and I'm having a blast working with you!"

"Awww, thanks Michelle."

Angie interjected, "Why don't you two do a little of your journalist sleuthing and see if you can find out where they are doing the release."

"That's a good idea," replied Caleb. "Are you still in touch with your friends on the release team?"

"I am as a matter of fact, maybe I could have coffee with Lainie and see if she knows anything."

"Cool, give her a call! Otherwise today is going to be a bust."

"Okay, I'll see what I can do."

Angie was the first to notice snowflakes drifting lazily down from the steel gray skies, as the trio emptied the last of the coffee.

"It's starting to snow," she said.

"According to the weather we are supposed to have a few inches on the ground by this afternoon," replied Michelle.

Caleb walked over to the sliding glass doors and stared out the window..

"Guess I'll lace up my snowshoes," he commented.

Michelle and Angie giggled a little and Angie said, "We knew you were going to say that!"

"Yeah, we knew you couldn't resist the snow."

"I guess I do have a soft spot for falling snow."

Caleb slipped out the sliding doors with his camera while Michelle called her friend Lainie.

Angie busied herself with some new fashion products and Michelle commented, "Lainie is off work today, so I'm going to run up to the bookstore for coffee with her before the snow gets too bad."

"Okay honey, drive safe. It could get slippery today."

Lainie was already sitting at a table when Michelle arrived. Lainie was a beautiful young woman with shining jet black hair.

"*She is dressed like a movie star,*" Michelle thought to herself. "*I wonder if she'd be interested in working with Angie and Jessie?*"

Lainie stood to give Michelle a hug, "Hi Michelle, it's been a long time!"

"It has, it's so good to see you," said Michelle as she reached for a hug.

"Well, should we go order something?"

They walked together to the counter to place their orders and Lainie said, "I heard you quit the park service."

"Yeah, I couldn't stand the gate anymore. I asked for a new assignment but got the standard answer, budget cuts, talks underway, maybe next year, blah, blah, blah."

"They do have an infuriating habit of making excuses."

"How has work been for you?"

"Oh pretty good, did you hear we have some wolves from British Columbia to release this month?"

"I just saw that this morning. Are you on the release team again?"

"I am."

"Do you know where and when they are going to do the release?"

"We have fifteen wolves, so we are going to release them in groups of five somewhere west of the Divide."

"I would love to be there, do you think they would mind if Caleb and I showed up?"

"I don't know, I'll ask around. I don't see why you couldn't be there. If not, maybe you could snowshoe into the vicinity."

"Oh, that would be amazing Lainie!"

The two old friends took their drinks back to their table to catch up on each other's lives. In the meantime Caleb returned from his snowshoe hike, with a batch of pictures of fresh fallen snow.

"Where's Michelle?" he asked.

"She went to have coffee with Lainie."

"Did she say if Lainie was going to tell her anything?"

"No, she just said she would be back in a while."

"Okay, I guess I'll just have to wait," he said as he pulled the memory card out of his camera.

Angie was in her room working on a new fashion design and Caleb had nodded off to sleep when Michelle burst through the front door, along with a blast of freezing air and a flurry of snow. A startled Caleb awoke and took a deep breath as he tried to jolt himself back to consciousness.

"It's getting bad out there!" Michelle exclaimed.

"Oh hey Michelle," Caleb replied. "How did your meeting go?"

"It was more just a cup of coffee than a meeting, but it was good. Lainie says she is going to ask around to see if we can get an invite."

"When are they going to release them?"

"It turns out they have fifteen wolves, and they are going to release them five at a time over the next couple of months."

"Awesome!" exclaimed Caleb.

"Oh good, you are home safe. It's getting bad out there," said Angie when she walked into the room.

"Michelle says Lainie is going to try to get us into the release."

"That's great Caleb, how is Lainie anyway?"

"She's fine, looking like a a million bucks as usual. You should try to recruit her into your business!"

"Has she ever indicated an interest?"

"No, I guess not. But I'm not sure she really knows what you are up to. Maybe you can fill her in at the release, whenever it is."

"Okay, I really don't know her but maybe we'll hit it off."

"I know you'll like her."

Angie commented, "I'm done with my work for the day, anyone up for some hot buttered rum?"

"Oh, that sounds really good on a cold day," replied Michelle.

"It does, and I need a break from this article. It has almost put me in a coma," laughed Caleb.

As the storm raged outside, the little group was snuggled on the couch watching a movie. Snow fell heavily for the rest of the night, and into the next day. Three feet covered the ground by the time the sun began to show through the cloud cover a day later.

Caleb was lacing up his tall boots when Michelle and Angie awoke. As Angie poured a cup of coffee she asked, "Where are you going Caleb?"

"I'm going out to shovel."

"Want some help?"

"No thanks, I got it."

Michelle burst through the front door as Caleb tossed another shovel full off the driveway.

"Caleb, we're in!"

"We're in what?" asked Caleb as he stopped shoveling to wipe the sweat off his forehead.

"The release, it's happening Friday and we get to be there!"

"That's awesome Michelle! I guess that means I have two days to shovel all this snow off the driveway," he laughed.

"Let me know if you need help," she offered.

"I think I'm going to take a break, and I'm going to need some aspirin."

"I'll bet," she replied.

"How about a beer," Angie offered as Caleb came in and sat down.

"That sounds really good right now," replied Caleb.

"Jessica and I have a meeting on Friday, so if it's okay with you it will be just you and Michelle going to the release."

Caleb rubbed his neck and replied, "We will miss you, but I know you and Jessie are busy."

"Make sure you get some good pictures and video so we can all watch it!"

"We will."

"We need to be there pretty early Friday morning, so we should probably stay over in Leadville on Thursday night," commented Michelle.

"Yeah, we can go shopping for snacks and stuff tomorrow," replied Caleb. "Is Thursday okay with you Angie?"

"Of course Caleb. You might want to get reservations, ski season is in full swing."

Caleb and Michelle rolled into Leadville just before the dinner hour and Caleb said, "Let's get checked in and go find something to eat."

"Sounds great Caleb, I'm starving."

"I guess we should get to bed early, we need to be on the road by five tomorrow morning."

"Yeah, I'm beat anyway."

Lainie greeted her friends as they climbed out of Caleb's truck.

"Glad you guys could make it!"

"We wouldn't miss this for anything," beamed Michelle.

"Oh I know, isn't this exciting?"

"Can we see the wolves?" asked Caleb.

"Sure, they are right over here in the cages. We are making sure they haven't had any ill effects from the ride out here."

"These don't look any different than the Elk Creek wolves."

"No, why would they?"

"All I've been hearing is how these giant Canadian wolves are going to eat all the elk and deer."

Lainie replied, "The ranchers are just spreading BS to scare the public. There's no such thing as a Canadian wolf, they are all Canis lupus, gray wolves."

"I actually heard the ranchers have signed up some kind of artificial intelligence bots to flood all the social media posts with anti wolf propaganda."

"I heard that too," replied Lainie. "Can you believe it? You would think this is still 1926 the way they are freaking out."

"How do we combat that?"

"Just keep doing what your doing Caleb. Education is the key."

"Based on the posts I've been seeing, education isn't exactly a strong point for the hunting and ranching lobby. Makes me wonder if they hired illiterate bots on purpose."

Lainie laughed, "Yeah, they seem to have a limited grasp on grammar and basic math skills."

Caleb saw that they were getting ready to open the cages and warned Michelle, "It's showtime Michelle, is your camera ready?"

"I'm ready!"

"You got the video, I'm going to shoot the stills again."

Rangers pulled open the doors and the confused wolves tentatively exited their enclosures. They each looked at the others and gathered in a group as if they were making a plan. Once the animals realized they were no longer captive, they began trotting toward Caleb who was filming from the side, with a beautiful mountain vista in the background.

It was apparent that the smaller animals had recognized a large male as the group leader, and as he broke into a trot the others fell in behind. The alpha stopped for a second as he passed Caleb, as if asking permission to leave.

"Go on buddy, you're free," exclaimed Caleb as he waved the new pack on toward the wilderness.

The leader seemed to understand his words of encouragement, and broke into a full run with the other four animals right on his heels. Caleb filmed their dash to freedom until the last of them was completely out of sight.

Michelle rushed to Caleb's side as he stared into the mountains. He put his arm around her and pulled her close, “I hope these fare better than the Elk Creek wolves.”

“Me too Caleb.”

Indiscriminate Death

The massive Colorado snow pack had finally begun to melt, and Ember's pack was learning to fend for themselves. Their home in the lush Crystal River valley provided abundant food for the family, with both large and small prey readily available. Day by day the snow receded from the banks of the river, and Ember and her pups enjoyed long naps in the soft mountain grass and warm Colorado sunshine.

One morning as they were resting in the tall grass, a strange creature entered their domain. Ember's ears perked up, and she watched the creature with great curiosity. It wasn't a deer or elk calf, but it also wasn't a large animal with an intimidating rack of dangerous antlers. Why would such a small and docile looking ungulate have entered their hunting grounds undefended? Ember didn't know, and her instincts were only to feed her family. She had no idea this was a domestic calf, as there was no fence and no humans to provide a clue otherwise.

She trotted into the clearing to see how the animal would react and the little calf began to run. A wolf's instinct in that case is simple, chase and kill. The encounter was soon over and Ember and her pups were enjoying meal of fresh meat, blissfully unaware that they had just committed an unforgivable crime in they eyes of the rancher on the other side of the ridge.

No other stray cattle entered the valley for some time, and the Elk Creek Pack went back to hunting their normal wild prey. In the meantime, coyotes and crows picked the calf's carcass clean and carried away the bones. No evidence remained of the depredation, and none was found when ranch hands rode through the valley in search of the missing animal. Ember and her family were well aware of the danger posed by humans, and remained hidden until long after the search party had departed.

“What are you doing this morning?” Angie asked Caleb as he poured his morning coffee.

“I don't know, I guess I don't have any big plans.”

“Jessie is coming over, and we were hoping we could do a photoshoot for our spring fashions over in the canyon this morning.”

“Sure, give me a few minutes to charge up some batteries for my lighting gear.”

“You have a couple of hours, Jessie isn't coming over until about nine.”

Caleb picked up his coffee and disappeared into his walk-in closet to dig out his lighting kit.

“What's Caleb doing?” asked Michelle as she walked into the kitchen.

“We are going to do a spring photoshoot this morning over in the canyon, do you want to model some of the new designs?”

“I guess that would be okay. I doubt Caleb needs any help with this, other than carrying his equipment. Of course you are going to have stuff to carry as well.”

“Nothing heavy today. I don't think we'll even need the changing tent. Nobody is going to be in canyon today, and we can just change inside the old concrete foundation.”

With a crash and a bang, Caleb exited the closet and dragged his lighting gear out to his truck. Michelle ran along behind picking up various items that were falling out of his overstuffed bag.”

"You aren't really awake yet are you Caleb?" she laughed.

Caleb chuckled and replied, "No I really am not. I think I'll be okay after a couple more cups of coffee. Are you going to help me out this morning?"

"Too late, Angie already has dibs."

"Ahhh... so you are going to model then."

A car pulled into the driveway and Michelle said, "It's Jessie."

"Are you guys loading up for the photoshoot?" Jessie asked.

"We are," replied Caleb. "There's fresh coffee in the kitchen if you want some."

"Coffee would be amazing Caleb, thanks!"

As Caleb and Michelle drove through the north entrance to the park Michelle exclaimed, "Hey look, it's Heather in the booth!"

Michelle leaped out of the truck to gave Heather a big hug, as Caleb stopped to pull out his state parks pass.

"It has been so long, how have you been?"

Heather replied, "I've been well, how about you?"

"Just fine, thanks!"

"How do you like working for Caleb?"

"He's a pretty easy boss," laughed Michelle. "Caleb, you can go set up if you like. I'll ride down with Angie and Jessie when they get here."

Heather asked, "Have you been out west to check on the new wolves from Canada?"

"No, I haven't heard anything about them since the release."

"I've heard that people have been spotting one of them out by Leadville occasionally."

"Cool, maybe Caleb and I can make a scouting run."

"You should do it, Caleb would love to get some pictures! Oh and you too now that you are a big shot photographer!"

Michelle laughed, "I don't know about big shot. Caleb is teaching me all the tricks, but I'm a long way from calling myself a professional photographer."

"I'm sure you are learning fast!"

Angie and Jessie drove up just then and greeted Heather as well. Michelle hopped into the car and they slowly drove down to the concrete flood ruins.

Caleb was already there with one light on a stand, and a flash trigger attached to his camera. The three girls took turns modeling new fashions and climbing around on the ruins. Jessie especially liked climbing up into the big window frame for her shots, and Angie liked standing in the doorway. Michelle put on a western style denim outfit and posed by the split rail fence.

Eventually they had been through all the looks, and Angie suggested they go do a few poses on the stair step structure of the old dam. They loaded up their gear and clothing into their vehicles and headed south toward the old flood damaged dam. As they drove carefully along the creek bed Michelle said to Caleb, "Heather says there have been sightings of the new packs up near Leadville. We should go check it out!"

"That would be fine by me, I'm always up for a road trip. We can save money by camping up at Half Moon along the creek."

"Awesome, it should be a nice time of year for a camp out."

The girls enjoyed posing and climbing around on the dam ruins until Caleb mentioned that the midday light was becoming too harsh for good pictures.

"Okay let's pack it up then," suggested Angie. "I think we have plenty of pictures for today. Should we go up to the Stage Line and have a beer and some lunch?"

Jessie replied, "A beer would be amazing. I am so thirsty from working in the sun!"

"A short day of work and a beer, it doesn't get any better than this!" added Caleb.

Caleb told Angie of he and Michelle's plans for a road trip as the four friends sipped their beer.

"That's a great idea Caleb, how long will you be gone?"

"Just a couple days I think. Either the wolf is where Heather said, or it has moved on. There's no since randomly searching a thousand square miles for a wolf that might not be there anymore."

Caleb and Michelle were on the road early the next morning and Michelle asked, "What are we going to do first?"

"I think we'll hike back in along the Colorado Trail where they have been seeing the wolf. Maybe we can knock out our pictures on the first day!"

"Works for me!"

"We'll drive up 390 to Winfield and hike back toward Lulu Gulch. If we don't see anything within a couple hours, we'll drive around and head up Half Moon Road to the campground. I'll bet the creek is really roaring today!"

Caleb parked the truck and pulled their packs out of the bed. Soon they were walking toward the recent sightings in high spirits. Eventually they reached Clear Creek and put down their gear for a rest. Caleb reached into his pack to retrieve his water filter and said, "This seems like a good spot to fill our water bottles. The water is clear and cold, and not much debris."

Michelle replied, "Sounds good to me Caleb. I'm going to catch some rays while you do that."

Caleb walked down by the river to fill the water, and returned with a disturbed look on his face.

"What is it Caleb, what's wrong?"

"Do you hear that?"

"Yeah, sounds like a coyote yipping or something."

"Funny, it's not stopping and it's not moving."

"Coyotes don't hang around in one spot and cry, it's not my experience anyway."

"Let's go check it out," suggested Caleb.

The pair bushwhacked about fifty yards into the trees and encountered a horrifying scene. A man with a hammer was swinging it at a screaming canine of some kind.

"What the hell, is that a trapper?" asked Caleb.

"I don't know, I don't think trapping is legal in the national forest."

"Let's go stop him," said Caleb. "You distract him from the front and I'll circle back behind and see if I can get rid of that rifle standing beside the tree."

"Okay, are you ready?"

"Give me a one minute head start, and then start yelling at him. Make sure you get a picture of his ugly mug for identification."

Caleb disappeared into the forest to the south and Michelle checked the time on her phone. When sixty seconds had passed, she walked around to the east, directly in front of the trapper.

"Stop that!" she yelled.

The man stopped swinging the hammer and started cursing her, and she stood her ground as he began walking menacingly toward her. Caleb quietly moved in behind and threw the rifle over the edge of the hill into the other fork of the stream. He waved Michelle away and stood near the collared animal. He surmised it was one of the new British Columbia wolves, now lying on the ground bleeding and whining in pain.

"Hey," he yelled.

The trapper whirled around to confront Caleb, who was now circling the area just outside the trap line that had been placed around a deer carcass the trapper was using for bait. Caleb warned him to put down the hammer.

"What if I don't?"

"Then I'm going to use it on you. Now drop it!"

Still cursing profusely, the trapper moved toward Caleb who kept circling just outside the trap line. By now the man was completely enraged, and lunging at Caleb with the hammer. But Caleb was too quick for the grizzled old mountain man, who try as he might was unable to strike Caleb with the weapon. Soon Caleb heard a snap, and knew instantly that the trapper had stepped into one of his own devices.

As he fell backward, Caleb grabbed the hammer with his right hand and thumped the trapper in the chest with his other. The trapper went down screaming in pain, and Caleb rushed to the wolf's side.

"Michelle, hurry!" he exclaimed.

She quickly rushed to his side, and they examined the injured animal.

“He's hurt bad, I wonder how many times this idiot clubbed him.”

“I don't know, can you call somebody?”

Michelle checked her phone and replied, “I have zero bars here.”

“I don't have a signal either, and I don't have my sat phone today.”

“Okay, let's get a couple of good branches and make a stretcher with our jackets. We'll pull him out to the road as gently as we can.”

In the meantime the trapper was still yelling and cursing, demanding to be released from the trap.

“What are you worried about,” commented Caleb. “You are always telling everyone how humane those traps are. Someone will be along eventually to release you. I hope you have to lay here as long as this poor animal did. Consider yourself lucky that I don't have time to stick around and beat you with your hammer.”

The trapper continued to spew filth from his vile lips as Caleb and Michelle began transporting the wolf back to the truck. After about fifteen difficult minutes, Caleb heard Michelle cry out, “Caleb, we're losing him!”

Caleb put down the sticks and rushed to the animal's side. The wolf was breathing hard and appeared to be seizing. Caleb tried massaging big canine's chest to no avail, and soon the seizure was over and the wolf was no longer breathing. Caleb tried for several minutes to resuscitate the beautiful wolf, until he heard Michelle's voice, “Caleb, he's gone.”

Caleb put his head on the animal's chest to check for a heartbeat, and after detecting none, he collapsed on top of the wolf while tears streamed down Michelle's face.

After several minutes of silence Caleb finally sat up and said, “Let's finish getting him out to the road and load him in the truck. We'll call the authorities when we can get a signal.”

“What about the trapper?”

“We can tell the wolf people where he is when they come to get the animal. I hope they put him in jail. Did you get a picture of him?”

“I got several. I'm sure they will be able to ID him if he somehow managed to get out of his trap.”

Death of a Pack

Just after sunrise on a beautiful Colorado mountain morning in May, Ember was awakened from her slumber in the peaceful Crystal River Valley as the sound of bellowing cattle echoed through the valley. The cattle were spreading out into their summer range on public land leased by the neighboring ranch. Her young ones were also soon startled out of their sleep, and the pack watched with great curiosity as their domain was invaded by the huge lumbering beasts.

It had been a few days since the young pack had enjoyed a major kill, when a doe mule deer suffering from wasting disease had stumbled into the valley. It had been a good breeding season for the cattle, and many calves accompanied their mothers as the livestock rotated into their summer range. Ember watched excitedly as a mother and her calf obliviously approached the wolf pack. The calf wandered several yards from it's mother and Ember saw her opportunity. She lunged at the calf and quickly ended it's life with a powerful bite to the neck.

The mother calf bellowed in dismay at the loss of her offspring, but the rest of the herd paid little attention. It was not an uncommon thing for a mother calf to bellow to her offspring to bring them back into her presence. Ember and her pups ate their fill and disappeared back into the trees for a nap. However their respite was soon interrupted by new invaders, cowboys on horseback whistling and yelling as they herded more cattle into the valley.

When the ranch hands heard the persistent bellowing of the grieving cow, one of the cowboys went to investigate. Finding the bloody carcass, he yelled out for the other cowboys to investigate.

"Hey, looks like we've got a wolf kill over here!!"

One of other cowboys rode up to examine the carcass and exclaimed, "It sure looks like a wolf kill, what do we do?"

"Give parks a call. They are supposed to investigate these things and reimburse us for the loss."

Colorado authorities were on the scene before the end of the day to make an initial assessment.

Ranch hands gathered around as the officials examined the scene.

One of the rangers spoke, "My initial assessment is that this incident appears to be a wolf kill. Of course we will have to gather these remains and take them back to the lab for a more thorough examination."

"Well when do we get our money?"

"These investigations take awhile. It could be a couple months before we can disperse funds."

"Well that's not acceptable. We are minus one calf right now."

"Well I'm sorry but you'll have to wait."

"But we are down a calf, we need to replace it."

"Don't give me that, you lose calves all the time to injury, exposure and disease. This is just one more calf, and you'll have to just deal with it like you would a lost calf for any other reason."

"Well we were told we'd be paid for our losses."

"If we determine that this was definitely a wolf attack, you will get your money in due time."

"What if we go to the media with this?"

"We can't stop you from talking to the media, but I'm asking you not to make a big deal out of this until we can determine what actually killed this animal."

"Well, the boss is going to do what he's going to do. I doubt he's going to care what you want."

"Do what you have to do, but I'm asking you to keep a lid on this until we publish our findings."

Wildlife officials completed their initial assessment and left the scene. Cowboys rode the perimeter of the valley looking for wolf sign, but finally gave up as dusk approached.

This scenario played out two more times, and each incident was met with more and more scrutiny in the valley.

On a late May morning in the crisp mountain air, the young pack spread out into the herd looking for a calf that might have wandered a bit too far from it's mother. One of Ember's pups discovered an opportunity and gave chase. But the chase ended with the terrifying crack of a rifle, and her pup fell dead in his tracks. Soon a team of wildlife officials was on the scene while Ember and her young pack scattered in fear. Colorado's first wolf pack since the extinction in the previous century, was no more.

Caleb returned from his morning run in the canyon and entered through the sliding glass doors. He was greeted by a grim faced Michelle who looked at him and said, "Caleb, I have some bad news."

"What is it, is everybody okay?"

"Oh, we're all fine but park officials have confirmed that they have shot and killed one of the Elk Creek pups. Chronic depredation is what they are calling it."

"What, what about the rest of the pack?"

"They don't seem to know but apparently they think they could identify the pup that was doing the killing, and they shot it. Early reports indicate the pack has scattered, and they don't know if they will come back together again."

"Well damn, I was afraid of that. These ranchers aren't cooperating and they probably make more money from a dead calf than a live one with the easy reimbursement policy published by the parks department."

"What are we going to do," asked Michelle.

"I don't know, I don't know if there's anything we can do."

"I suppose you are right."

Throughout that fateful summer, eleven more Colorado wolves had perished under varying circumstances. One was hit by a car, another shot by hunters in Wyoming. Others disappeared mysteriously with little transparency from Colorado officials.

Caleb was sipping coffee on a sunny August morning when Angie walked into the room yawning and stretching. She poured herself a cup of coffee and sat down at the table.

"Good morning, did you get enough sleep?" asked Caleb.

"I had a little trouble falling asleep, but I'm good. How about you?"

"I'm good, just trying to figure out what I'm going to do today."

"Can you believe it's August already?"

"I know right? It seems like it was just snowing a week ago."

"It wasn't a week ago, but we did get a foot of snow in the middle of June. That wasn't that long ago!"

"True, and the way it is around here we could have snow again in a few weeks."

"Yeah, but it won't stick."

"I know, but once it starts..." said Caleb, his voice trailing off.

"Jessie and I will be announcing our fall fashion line soon. Are you up for a photoshoot?"

"Sure, where are we going to do it?"

"I don't know, maybe someplace with a nice mountain backdrop."

"I suppose I could get a permit for Rocky Mountain National Park. They finally passed the Explore Act, so we could probably shoot in various locations on the east side with the continental divide in the background. I wouldn't be able to set up a bunch of light stands, but we should be able to figure something out."

"That sounds nice Caleb, I'll talk to Jessie and see when she can go."

"Cool, just give a a couple days notice so I can prepare."

Michelle was the last to awaken, and also poured herself a cup of coffee.

"What are we talking about this morning?"

"Angie wants to do a photoshoot for her fall line. I was thinking we could do it in Rocky."

"That sounds like fun, are we going to camp out?"

"I guess we could, what do you think Angie?"

"Camping would be nice, I'll see if Jessie wants to."

"What are you up to on this fine morning?" Caleb asked Michelle.

"I don't know, I was thinking about going back home to see Mom again."

"Do you want some company?" asked Caleb.

"Sure, you wouldn't mind driving out with me?"

"Yeah, we could stop and see the wild horses and hit the Lamar Valley along the way. Is that okay with you Angie?"

"It's okay with me, as long as we get our photoshoot done first."

"What do you think about waiting until after the Labor Day weekend?" Caleb asked Michelle.

"That's a good idea, the tourist season will be winding down."

"Sounds like a plan," commented Caleb. "Would you want to go too Angie?"

"Maybe," she replied. "We haven't seen my family in a while, I'm sure they'd be happy to see us."

"I see another one of the British Columbia wolves has died in Pitkin County," commented Caleb.

"How?" asked Michelle.

"I don't know, they aren't saying."

"Probably shot by a rancher. Why isn't the parks department arresting anybody?" she asked.

"I don't know," replied Caleb. "They seem to be afraid to take on the ranching lobby."

"I wouldn't have voted for wolves if I had known parks was just going to let ranchers and hunters kill them all. What's the sense of that?"

"I don't know, maybe we need a new director," replied Caleb. "Have you seen the vile comments online?"

"No, what are they saying?"

"Mostly the same thing over and over, God they are stupid."

"It seems like AI, flooding the zone with anti-wolf propaganda."

"It probably is. I've responded to a few of the more stupid people and they never reply or even try to defend themselves. And if they do reply, it's just with an infuriating smiley face."

"That's an easy response for an AI bot," replied Michelle.

Caleb chuckled and muttered, "Artificial Stupidity."

'Yeah."

Angie received a text and picked up her phone.

"Jessie thinks a camping trip in the park sounds like fun."

"All right then, how about next week?" suggested Caleb.

"Works for me," replied Michelle.

"Next week it is then," added Angie.

Mountain Fashion

The group rolled into Estes Park around lunchtime and found the campground to check in. After Caleb paid the fee Angie asked, "Should we set up camp before we get involved with shooting?"

Caleb replied, "That would probably be the best thing. We'll have better light for photography later when the sun is a bit lower in the sky."

They quickly found their site and began unloading the tent and sleeping bags.

"Michelle do you want to help me set up the tent while Angie and Jessie unload the rest of the gear?"

"Sure, what do you need me to do?"

"I'll stake it down if you want to assemble the poles."

"I can do that!"

"Soon the tent was was set up with sleeping bags and pillows inside. Jessica asked if they should start a campfire.

"Maybe later, what do you say we take a little drive into town first? Do you girls have some urban fashions to show off?"

Angie replied, "As a matter of fact we do! Let's go over to the restrooms and try some on."

Soon they were dressed and rolling into Estes Park.

Caleb asked, "Should we get some lunch while we're in town?"

"That's a great idea Caleb, I'm starving," commented Michelle.

They followed the directions to the free parking lot on the west end of town and found a parking place. Caleb got out his camera and speed light and snapped a couple of pictures of the women as they strolled along the banks of beautiful Fall River.

"We can also get some pictures of you ladies in front of these colorful shops, if you don't mind," commented Caleb.

Angie and Jessica were enjoying the walk immensely, posing and twirling occasionally so Caleb could get pictures. They soon came upon a nice looking deli advertising sandwiches and beer.

"How about this place?" asked Caleb.

"This looks good," commented Jessica.

The others nodded and they went on inside to get a table.

As they waited for their orders, Caleb heard people at the next table talking about a wolf that was found dead in Colorado. He asked them what they had heard and was surprised at the answer.

"Yes, apparently they picked up a mortality signal over on the west side of the park. When they went to check it out, one of the new wolves from British Columbia was found deceased."

"Do they know what happened?"

"They are being pretty tight lipped as usual, only saying that there will be an investigation although we did hear rumors that it might be a mountain lion attack."

When Caleb turned back around Angie asked, "What is it Caleb, what are they talking about?"

Caleb replied, "One of our new Canadian wolves was found dead on the other side of the park."

"How?"

"Nobody knows for sure yet, but some are saying it was a mountain lion."

"This has been a rough summer for the wolf program hasn't it?"

"Yes it has."

"There's also a rumor that the feds are going to step in and stop the Colorado reintroduction program."

"Seriously?" exclaimed Michelle.

"Well, that's what these people heard anyway," replied Caleb.

"President Turner and his interior guy have it in for Colorado, especially the governor. I wouldn't be surprised if there was some kind of vindictiveness going on in the backrooms," added Angie.

After a few seconds of silence Jessica asked, "What are we going to do after lunch?"

Caleb replied, “I thought we might shoot a few more pictures in town, then maybe head up to Sprague Lake. There's some cool wooden walkways there that we can use as props, and Otis and Hallet peaks will look amazing in the background. How does that sound?”

“Works for me!”

Angie exclaimed, “I like it too!”

“I go where you go,” laughed Michelle.

They finished a leisurely lunch and wandered back out into the street. Jessica spotted some colorful umbrellas in a nearby shop window and exclaimed, “Wouldn't those umbrellas make great props?”

Angie replied, “They sure would, let's go in and grab a couple! Michelle, you should get one too!”

“We'll see,” she replied.

The eclectic group whiled away the day shopping, hiking, and shooting a few looks that Angie had packed in her day bag. Eventually the sun sagged low in the sky, and the temperature dropped precipitously along the shores of the ice cold alpine lake.

“Wow, it's getting chilly, should we head back into town?” asked Angie.

Caleb replied, “Sure, maybe we should get some firewood and have a campfire tonight.”

Michelle added, “Why don't we get some of that smooth whiskey we had up at Steamboat!”

"We can grab a bottle of that, and maybe some marshmallows to toast."

Soon they were back at camp, with Caleb rummaging around in the back of the SUV for the camp chairs. Angie brought out some paper cups while Michelle popped the cork on the bottle of whiskey.

"Be careful of this stuff, it might make your clothes fall off, especially you Jessie!" warned Michelle.

Jessica laughed, "What, my clothes don't fall off."

Angie chuckled, "Jessie doesn't need whiskey for her clothes to fall off.

"Shut up," she laughed.

Soon the four partners were gathered around a beautiful flickering fire, enjoying smooth whiskey and toasting marshmallows on sticks. Caleb was fiddling with his phone when he commented, "Michelle, remember that gregarious wolf we were watching in the Lamar Valley?"

"Yeah the female, 1479 right?"

"That's the one. Apparently she was shot by a hunter waiting outside the park boundary."

"Oh damn that's a shame, she was fun. There's a special place in hell for those hunters targeting Yellowstone wildlife."

Caleb replied, "Yes there is, may God Himself take vengeance on their wicked souls."

"Maybe the wolves will start eating hunters," muttered Michelle.

"Don't these people feel any guilt about shooting these beloved animals?" asked Jessica.

"I don't think so, in fact they seem to think they are on some kind of mission to kill any animal they think is competition for their twisted way of life. They think somehow they are in a holy war against anyone who wants wild animals alive," replied Caleb.

There was a long pause as all four stared into the flames. It was Angie who finally broke the silence, "I'm thinking of having a Thanksgiving party. Some of our girls don't have anywhere to go, and I think it would be nice to have them over."

Jessica replied, "That's a great idea Angie, let's get it done! My stupid husband will have all his football buddies over and I sure don't want to be their personal waitress."

"We could have some champagne to celebrate our new agency, along with turkey and fixings."

Michelle added, "That will be really nice Angie, let me know what I can do to help."

"Thanks honey, we'll figure it out when the time comes. What about you Caleb, you are awful quiet tonight."

"Oh, it sounds great Angie! You always put on a beautiful party."

"What's the matter, I can tell when something is bothering you."

Caleb thought for a while, "You know, I think I'm just tired. I'm tired of all the death, all the hate. I'm tired of fighting self-entitled whining ranchers and ignorant trophy hunters, and it never seems to do any good. They don't listen, can't learn, and then they just get mad and start with the name calling when they know they are losing an argument. I wonder if maybe I've taken this wildlife advocacy thing as far as I can."

"Oh no, if you quit now the pigs win," replied Michelle.

Caleb responded with an unintelligible grunt.

"All those horrible people we've been fighting the last few years, the blood thirsty murdering hunters, the lying ranchers who make up all the hate filled stories about wolves, like the stupid "huge Canadian subspecies" narrative, and "the wolves are going to eat all the deer and kill all the cattle" bullshit stories. And what about the politicians, who are in bed with the ranchers and developers, and want to give all the public land away. And the lying psychotic trappers who spread insane stories about how they are "managing" wildlife, and telling ridiculous lies about humane trapping. And who's going to do the reporting, who will tell the stories about the hunters killing all the Yellowstone animals when they take one step out of the park? If you don't stand up for the animals, who will? What kind of example are you going to make for your followers if you quit, what will they think? And not only that I just came to work for you, what about me? What would I do if you quit?" exclaimed Michelle.

Angie replied, "Caleb isn't going to give up on the wildlife, he cares too much about them to quit. I think he's just a little tired from all the killing this year."

Caleb smiled, "That was quite a soul stirring speech! You have me convinced. Of course we aren't going to give up, and I'm going to have plenty more work for you. We're going to give them hell!"

"That's more like it, that's the Caleb I know!" exclaimed Michelle.

"Why don't you and Michelle join me and Jessie part time, maybe take some of the pressure off and lighten things up a bit. Maybe you could take a little time off from writing books and do more photography for a while. Didn't you start out as a fashion photographer out in the Bay Area?"

"That's right I did., I got Lacey her start out there."

"What made you quit?"

"Lacey got her big break and moved to New York City, and I didn't enjoy the City anymore after she left. I started dreaming of the mountains, call of the wild I guess."

"But you still enjoy fashion photography right?"

As Caleb stared into the fire, a distant gaze took him back in time to another place, where the glowing embers became the city lights of his youth.

"You know... I do kind of miss the studio I had in Cupertino. I enjoyed just sitting in my office chair after a days work, staring out at the city lights. I was just getting my start, and the lights inspired me."

Angie stared into his face and tried to imagine his life before Montana. She knew he had come from the San Francisco area, but had never really given much thought to his life there.

After a long silence Caleb commented, "I wonder if we should open a real studio?"

Angie lovingly replied, "Maybe so Caleb, maybe so."

The four friends watched in silence as the glowing coals gradually faded into the final moments of that fateful season.

Epilogue

The third installment of this wildlife saga ends with a blend of despair and hope. The Colorado wolf reintroduction program has gotten off to a rough start. The Copper Creek Pack from the original release has been decimated by the death of two of it's members, including the breeding male. All together, 14 of 25 released wolves are now dead due to various and sometimes mysterious circumstances.

The killing of Yellowstone's popular wolf 1479 mentioned in this book, was followed by the illegal poaching of her sister, wolf 1478 on Christmas Day in 2025. In 2026 alone, 24 wolves have already been killed in Wyoming's trophy hunting season. A statewide quota of 450 wolves is allowed in Montana, which is not a quota at all, but an appalling plan for total eradication.

Any mention of wolves on social media is met with an avalanche of visceral hatred and vile threats against their lives by an assortment of hunters, trappers and ranchers. Any comments in favor of protection for wolves are immediately drowned in a sea of vicious stereotyping and name calling. Any hint of limits placed on the killing of wildlife is met with defiance and resolve to continue the slaughter, regardless of new laws that might preserve the lives wild creatures.

Wild horses in the west continue to be persecuted by the BLM at the behest of cattle ranchers and sheepherders. Cruel helicopter roundups are still common, resulting in the maiming and death of many of these majestic and iconic animals. Although organizations exist that are dedicated to rescue and refuge of these horses, their efforts will not be sufficient to prevent the destruction of wild herds on public land.

The current administration is especially hostile toward wild horses, and if something isn't done to preserve public management ranges, wild horses will cease to exist in our lifetimes.

Ranching, sportsmen's rights, and property rights proponents are a very powerful, well funded, and influential force at both state and federal levels in the United States, and they have succeeded in ending endangered species protections for wolves in the Rocky Mountain West. The Endangered Species Act has never been more threatened than it is now, under a new republican administration and secretary of the interior that are overtly hostile toward our public lands and wild animals.

The wanton slaughter of so called nuisance animals such as prairie dogs, has left the landscape littered with toxic lead bullet fragments, and our raptors are dying in alarming numbers from ingesting carcasses filled with the poisonous metal.

Fur bearing animals are cruelly trapped with impunity and without limit, using various barbaric steel traps and snares including conibear devices that indiscriminately terminate the life of any animal that becomes ensnared in them, including dogs, raptors, and any other living being unfortunate enough to fall victim to such evil.

In some western states no limits at all are placed on methods used to kill predators, including cruel snares and even snowmobiles. Fortunately, in an event described in this book, one particular incident resulted in widespread awareness and worldwide condemnation of the practice, and is finally bringing change to the way predator animals are treated. As of this writing, prosecutors have successfully argued that wildlife has certain rights to humane treatment, and we await the final sentencing of the perpetrator of that now infamous incident.

However dire the situation now looks, hope is on the horizon. Over 100 countries around the world have banned trapping for being non-selective and inhumane. Many states in the U.S., have severely restricted trapping, with California enacting a total ban. Inhumane trail hunting has finally been outlawed in Great Britain, and hound hunting for bears has been banned in many states, including California, Colorado, Oregon, and Washington. Colorado, one of the worst offenders for wanton killing of small fur bearing animals, is now considering rule changes that would reclassify fur bearing animals such that state laws currently in existence can limit the slaughter.

Many countries have recently implemented total bans on trophy hunting to protect wildlife, including Kenya, Costa Rica, Malawi, Colombia, India, and South Sudan. More than thirty countries have enacted sentient being laws, recognizing animals as living beings with feelings and emotions rather than simple property. Some courts now consider pets as family members rather than property to be divided in divorce cases.

In a token step in the right direction, cruelty toward domestic animals is now a felony in the U..S., although the government needs to extend the benefit to wild animals as well. Many countries around the world are also taking steps to end the mistreatment of animals, including bans on dog and horse meat.

Even though the current situation for wildlife in America is atrocious, public awareness is on the increase and the tide has turned against organizations and individuals who wish to do harm to our wild living legacy. There are dozens of reputable organizations dedicated to the protection and humane treatment of wild and domestic animals, and each one of us can make a difference by joining and donating to one or more of them.

It is my sincere hope that this series of historical fiction novels, including prequels ***S**pirit of the Wolf* and *Thundering Hooves*, has made a difference in each of my reader's lives and shined a light upon the plight of our wild animals and our precious public lands.

I like my character Caleb in the trilogy, am weary of the fighting and heartbreak but it is my intention to continue increasing public awareness about the way our wild legacy is treated. I don't know if I will add to the trilogy, but I will continue to publish informative articles in my blog, and other outlets that may be applicable. And of course my cast of fictional characters are ready to spring back into action if the need arises!

Good luck and Godspeed fellow wildlife warriors!

Books by This Author

Thundering Hooves: Spirit of the West: Learn the inspiring story of Colorado's Sand Wash Basin wild horse herd in the inspiring second installment of this wildlife trilogy.

Spirit of the Wolf: Forever Wild, Eternally Free: Learn the thrilling and inspiring story of Yellowstone National Park's first wild wolves and their famous matriarch in over a century, following their extinction in the early 1900s, as they struggle for life and freedom in a harsh and hostile environment. Also meet and learn to love the gallant characters of this trilogy as they come of age and lead the way through many thrilling adventures, trials, tribulations, love, loss and triumph.

Storm Warning: How to Photograph the Rocky Mountain Winter: Learn how to capture beautiful images and survive the harsh Rocky Mountain winter in this beautiful photo book, including dozens of full color images of beautiful landscapes and wildlife, complete with detailed tutorials, including personal insights from the author.

Wildlife Photography in the Colorado Rockies: Both novice and experienced photographers will learn to shoot Rocky Mountain wildlife like a pro with these practical and easy to learn techniques. Amateurs and pros alike will appreciate this straight forward approach to finding and photographing wildlife in the beautiful Rocky Mountains of Colorado.

Two Decades of Digital Photography: Go on a 20 year journey of exciting photo adventures with the author in this beautiful photo book, including the author's memoirs and dozens of beautiful color images.

Seasons of the Raptor: A beautifully photographed tale of one year in the life of Colorado's iconic raptors, including eagles, hawks and osprey.

www.ingramcontent.com/pod-product-compliance
Lightning Source LLC
LaVergne TN
LVHW050615100826
845148LV00011B/1604

* 9 7 9 8 9 8 6 0 7 6 6 6 9 *